KT-497-107

Through the Water Curtain

& other Tales from Around the World

3800 18 0043234 0

HIGH LIFE HIGHLAND

m

PUSHKIN
CHILDREN'S

Through
the Water
Curtain

& other Tales
from Around
the World

Selected and
Introduced by

Cornelia
Funke

HIGH LIFE HIGHLAND LIBRARIES	
38001800432340	
BERTRAMS	29/10/2018
	£12.99
JF	

Pushkin Press
71–75 Shelton Street
London WC2H 9JQ

Introduction and glosses © Cornelia Funke 2018
English translations of "The Six Swans" and "Golden Foot" © Oliver Latsch 2018

First published by Pushkin Press in 2018

9 8 7 6 5 4 3 2 1

ISBN 13: 978-1-78269-200-3

All rights reserved. No part of this publication may be reproduced, stored in a retrieval system or transmitted in any form or by any means, electronic, mechanical, photocopying, recording or otherwise, without prior permission in writing from Pushkin Press

Designed and typeset by Tetragon, London
Printed and bound by CPI Group (UK) Ltd, Croydon CR0 4YY

www.pushkinpress.com

Contents

Introduction

I didn't like fairy tales when I was a child. No. I had a scratched LP (yes, that's how old I am) that contained several tales of the Brothers Grimm. I definitely recall *Cinderella*. Then there was the terrifying *Goose Maid*, with the chopped-off talking head of Falada, the faithful horse (utterly traumatizing), *King Thrushbeard*, *The Frog Prince*, *Hansel and Gretel*, *The Wolf and the Seven Goatlings*... I grew up in Germany, so the narrator read the original tales—abbreviated, I am sure, but not censored or modified to make them more digestible for children. I therefore knew the darker versions by heart before I encountered the interpretations of Walt Disney or the light-hearted Czech movie adaptations I learnt to love.

All that darkness was of course deeply troubling, but as the tales were both bewildering and strangely unforgettable, I listened to that LP almost every night in my bed, over and over again. It taught me how strange an enchantment fairy tales can cast even though the characters stay rather abstract and the plot takes the wildest and often very abrupt twists and turns. Fairy tales break all the rules of a good story and yet they find such powerful images for the deepest human emotions and fears that we sense deep layers of meaning in a poisonous apple or the gruelling setting of a gingerbread house, and more truth than a thousand words would grant.

Of course, that's an explanation I came up with much later for the lure of the scratchy LP. As a child I didn't ask myself what cast the spell. We accept the rules of enchanted lands much more easily when we are young.

Apart from the Grimm's LP, I also remember a book of *Hans Christian Andersen's Tales* bound in blue linen, a pale green volume of animal tales that I still own. In some of those stories I felt more at home than in *The Grimm's Tales*, maybe because their tone was more familiar and less distant in time. I didn't know yet about the difference between folk tales passed on by nameless storytellers over the ages and fairy tales created by modern authors like H.C. Andersen, Oscar Wilde or Rudyard Kipling (it doesn't get much better than *Just So Stories*).

Nevertheless. The dark tales the Grimms had collected, though so much older than *The Ugly Duckling* or *The Happy Prince*, stayed with me, along with their mysterious and powerful imagery, their archetypes and the magic of rose-covered castles and shoes filled with blood... which sometimes included a cut-off toe. But I probably still would've shaken my head in disbelief at the age of thirty if someone had told me that one day I'd own quite a collection of fairy-tale books, and I probably would've accepted any bet that I'd never make them a vital part of my own writing. Even when I was reading and rereading tales from all over the world for this anthology, I often felt again what I felt as my six-year-old self: that I don't really like fairy tales.

Oh, all those helpless princesses and scheming old women, all those child-eating witches and stepmothers! Does any literary mirror reflect more unflinchingly, how cruelly women are judged and vilified when they rebel against the parts men want them to play? All over the world, fairy tales describe the golden cages and the punishment for the women who try to escape them. Of course, in most cases the only hope for the heroine is the timely appearance of the prince. Folk and fairy tales tend to be quite reactionary. They don't even try to hide their purpose of confirming and preserving the values of patriarchal societies, with their strict hierarchies anchored by property and armed violence. But from time to time one comes across a tale with a slightly more rebellious message, and each time I discover one of those I wonder whether many others were forgotten exactly because they don't reaffirm the traditional values that even the liberal Grimms believed in.

Sometimes these rebellious tales may have their origin in older times, when women often inherited power because the men tended to get themselves killed quite young. Others have such powerful heroines that I suspect them to be the echoes of long-forgotten goddesses—or of a very rebellious witch. Even some familiar tales, like *Little Red Riding Hood*, have older versions with far less helpless heroines. And *Sleeping Beauty* was not always woken with just a kiss.

What about the happy ending? The older tales often don't have one, but even the Grimms did not just collect the tales they heard from oral storytellers. They censored and changed them according to their own values, which were the ideals of the rising middle class in the nineteenth century. The intentions were only the best, of course. Who wanted to celebrate the values of a cruel and barbaric past ruled by despotic nobles, veiled in hunger, darkness and superstition, when civilization had finally arrived? So once again fairy tales were told to confirm social values—even the hero who yearns for foreign lands and wild adventures will always come home to a wife who wishes for nothing but children and a husband to protect her.

Yes, fairy tales are time machines. They have preserved all the fears and hopes of our ancestors in the folds of their magical cloaks. They make their readers (or listeners) travel through long-vanished landscapes and meet long-dead kings, queens and gods. They remind us how dark the nights once were and how frightening a forest could be even in the bright light of the full moon. Maybe that is one explanation why these tales still cast a spell, although they so often reflect values that make us shudder. Who doesn't want to travel in time?

There is also another quality about them. Fairy tales are very honest about the darkness that nests in the human soul. The heroes want power, riches and the most beautiful girl. That's true at least of Western tales. In the East we may meet a king who becomes a hermit in the end. Or one who is punished by being turned into a woman and actually likes it.

Mirrors... When I let my hero step through a mirror for the first time in my first *Reckless* book—the series in which I follow a path of breadcrumbs stolen from fairy tales all over the world—some adults asked me why the tales are so dark. (Children rarely ask that question, maybe because they have a more realistic perception of the world.) I always reply that the darkness found in my books pales in comparison to the cruelty of the original tales. Cannibalism, incest, mutilation and murder...

Luckily there is often a magical object available that brings people back to life or most heroes would be dead after a few pages!

Maybe another aspect that explains the timeless enchantment these strange tales hold is that life and death are shown as two sides of the same coin. The circle of life, the power of nature, the awareness of being part of a web that includes every living thing on this planet, be it plant, animal or human, and the awareness that this net isn't torn by death—we are so estranged from nature that we have forgotten these truths. In fairy tales animals become humans, and humans wear fur or feathers—or turn into a tree. The world is still whole, not yet remade and defined by humanity. There is no illusion that we can control the wildness of this planet. There is no separation between man and animal, man and plant. The loneliness of modern man, our perception that we are the masters and manipulators of the planet that gave birth to us... we only find that in modern tales.

So, no, I don't like fairy tales. Yet some still enchant me profoundly. For in their imagery of monsters and magical things they preserve many forgotten truths. Sometimes we lost the key to decipher them but the images kept their power nevertheless. Try it! Whenever you travel, read a fairy tale from the region or the country you go to. I promise that they are very interesting travel guides. They'll hand you a skin to walk in that'll make you feel like a local. You may even learn more about the place than some of its residents remember!

Oh, yes, what made me choose the tales you'll find in this book? I let them come to me like magical creatures that cross our path in a labyrinth. Some I found while working on *Reckless* and they made me take a path I hadn't foreseen. Some I only discovered when I searched my library for tales that were a bit more rebellious than many of their famous siblings. Others came to me because I wanted this collection to make the reader travel through both familiar and unfamiliar fairy-tale territories. So one could say that chance guided me, curiosity, the wish for less-trodden roads, the love for rebellious heroes and heroines, the eye of the illustrator—who of course was enchanted by the boy drawing cats... As you see, finding these tales was a fairy-tale quest of its own.

—CORNELIA FUNKE

The Boy
Who Drew
Cats

long, long time ago, in a small country village in Japan, there lived a poor farmer and his wife, who were very good people. They had a number of children, and found it very hard to feed them all. The elder son was strong enough when only fourteen years old to help his father; and the little girls learnt to help their mother almost as soon as they could walk.

But the youngest child, a little boy, did not seem to be fit for hard work. He was very clever—cleverer than all his brothers and sisters—but he was quite weak and small, and people said he could never grow very big. So his parents thought it would be better for him to become a priest than to become a farmer. They took him with them to the village temple one day, and asked the good old priest who lived there if he would have their little boy for his acolyte and teach him all that a priest ought to know.

The old man spoke kindly to the lad, and asked him some hard questions. So clever were the answers that the priest agreed to take the little fellow into the temple as an acolyte and to educate him for the priesthood.

The boy learnt quickly what the old priest taught him, and was very obedient in most things. But he had one fault. He liked to draw cats during study hours, and to draw cats even where cats ought not to have been drawn at all.

Whenever he found himself alone, he drew cats. He drew them on the margins of the priest's books, and on all the screens of the temple, and on the walls, and on the pillars. Several times the priest told him this was not right; but he did not stop drawing cats. He drew them because he could not really help it. He had what is called "the genius of an *artist*", and just for that reason he was not quite fit to be an acolyte; a good acolyte should study books.

One day, after he had drawn some very clever pictures of cats upon a paper screen, the old priest said to him severely: "My boy, you must go away from this temple at once. You will never make a good priest, but perhaps you will become a great artist. Now let me give you a last piece of advice, and be sure you never forget it. *Avoid large places at night; keep to small!*"

The boy did not know what the priest meant by saying, "*Avoid large places; keep to small.*" He thought and thought, while he was tying up his little bundle of clothes to go away, but he could not understand those words, and he was afraid to speak to the priest any more, except to say goodbye.

He left the temple very sorrowfully, and began to wonder what he should do. If he went straight home he felt sure his father would punish him for having been disobedient to the priest: so he was afraid to go home. All at once he remembered that at the next village, twelve miles away, there was a very big temple. He had heard there were several priests at that temple, and he made up his mind to go to them and ask them to take him for their acolyte.

Now that big temple was closed up but the boy did not know this fact. The reason it had been closed up was that a goblin had frightened the priests away and had taken possession of the place. Some brave warriors had afterwards gone to the temple at night to kill the goblin; but they had never been seen alive again. Nobody had ever told these things to the boy, so he walked all the way to the village hoping to be kindly treated by the priests.

When he got to the village it was already dark, and all the people were in bed; but he saw the big temple on a hill at the other end of the principal street, and he saw there was a light in the temple. People who tell the story say the goblin used to make that light, in order to tempt lonely travellers to ask for shelter. The boy went at once to the temple, and knocked. There was no sound inside. He knocked and knocked again; but still nobody came. At last he pushed gently at the door, and was quite glad to find that it had not been fastened. So he went in, and saw a lamp burning—but no priest.

He thought some priest would be sure to come very soon, and he sat down and waited. Then he noticed that everything in the temple was grey with dust and thickly spun over with cobwebs. So he thought to himself that the priests would certainly like to have an acolyte, to keep the place clean. He wondered why they had allowed everything to get so dusty. What most pleased him, however, were some big white screens, good to paint cats upon. Though he was tired, he looked at once for a writing box, and found one, and ground some ink, and began to paint cats.

He painted a great many cats upon the screens, and then he began to feel very, very sleepy. He was just on the point of lying down to sleep beside one of the screens, when he suddenly remembered the words, "*Avoid large places; keep to small!*"

The temple was very large; he was all alone; and as he thought of these words—though he could not quite understand them—he began to feel for the first time a little afraid, and he resolved to look for a *"small place"* in which to sleep. He found a little cabinet with a sliding door, and went into it, and shut himself up. Then he lay down and fell fast asleep.

Very late in the night he was awakened by a most terrible noise—a noise of fighting and screaming. It was so dreadful that he was afraid even to look through a chink of the little cabinet: he lay very still, holding his breath for fright.

The light that had been in the temple went out; but the awful sounds continued, and became more awful, and all the temple shook. After a long time silence came; but the boy was still afraid to move. He did not move until the light of the morning sun shone into the cabinet through the chinks of the little door.

Then he got out of his hiding place very cautiously, and looked about. The first thing he saw was that all the floor of the temple was covered with blood. And then he saw, lying dead in the middle of it, an enormous, monstrous rat—a goblin-rat—bigger than a cow!

But who or what could have killed it? There was no man or other creature to be seen. Suddenly the boy observed that the mouths of all the cats he had drawn the night before were red and wet with blood. Then he knew that the goblin had been killed by the cats which he had drawn. And then also, for the first time,

21

he understood why the wise old priest had said to him, *"Avoid large places at night; keep to small."*

Afterwards that boy became a very famous artist. Some of the cats which he drew are still shown to travellers in Japan.

Well, it's quite obvious why this is one of my favourite fairy tales, isn't it? The illustrator in me wants to go to a lonely Japanese temple right now and draw cats onto the walls!

There is a familiar element: the youngest child who is considered quite useless, though in this case his father recognizes his cleverness. In European tales those young sons who turn out to be heroes are mostly described as dumb. But this hero from Japan is not our usual hero, who slays the monster and earns a crown and the princess. This hero learns about his talents as an artist, and the tale doesn't celebrate physical strength, cleverness, beauty or power. It celebrates the arts and the belief that what artists create holds the spark of life and can save us from monsters. I wish this tale were read at every school—to inspire some children to become heroes with a pen or brush. We need those so much more than the ones with a sword.

One note on the style of the narration. It is, of course, not the original Japanese tale; sadly I didn't find it. Lafcadio Hearn retells the story brilliantly and he definitely knows almost everything about Japan, but his tone is to my ears still the tone of a Western writer—which makes us aware of the fact that a fairy tale changes and shifts with every narrator who passes it on.

Kotura,
Lord of the
Winds

In a nomad camp in the wilds of the Far North lived an old man with his three daughters. The man was very poor. His choom barely kept out the icy wind and driving snow. And when the frost was keen enough to bite their naked hands and faces, the three daughters huddled together round the fire. As they lay down to sleep at night, their father would rake through the ashes; and then they would shiver throughout the long cold night till morning.

One day, in the depths of winter, a snowstorm blew up and raged across the tundra. It whipped through the camp the first day, then the second, and on into the third. There seemed no end to the driving snow and fierce wind. No bold Nenets dared show his face outside his tent and families sat fearful in their chooms, hungry and cold, dreading that the camp would be blown clean away.

The old man and his daughters crouched in their tent harking to the howling of the blizzard, and the father said:

"If the storm continues for much longer, we shall all die for certain. It was sent by Kotura, Lord of the Winds. He must be very angry with us. There's only one way to appease him and save the camp—we must send him a wife from our clan. You, my eldest daughter, must go to Kotura and beg him to halt the blizzard."

"But how am I to go?" asked the girl, in alarm. "I do not know the way."

"I shall give you a sled," said her father. "Turn your face into the north wind, push the sled forward and follow wherever it leads. The wind will tear open the strings that bind your coat; yet you must not stop to tie them. The snow will fill your shoes; yet you must not stop to shake it out. Continue on your way until you arrive at a steep hill; when you have climbed to the top, only then may you halt to shake the snow from your shoes and do up your coat.

"Presently, a little bird will perch on your shoulder. Do not brush him away, be kind and caress him gently. Then jump onto your sled and let it run down the other side of the hill. It will take you straight to the door of Kotura's choom. Enter and touch nothing; just sit patiently and wait until he comes. And do exactly as he tells you."

Eldest daughter put on her coat, turned the sled into the north wind and sent it gliding along before her.

She followed on foot and after a while the strings on her coat came undone, the swirling snow squeezed into her shoes and she was very, very cold. However, she did not heed her father's words: she stopped and began to tie the strings of her coat, to shake the snow from her shoes. That done, she moved on into the face of the north wind.

On and on through the snow she went until at last she came to a steep hill. And when she finally reached the top, a little bird flew down and would have alighted on her shoulder had she not waved her hands to shoo him away. Alarmed, the bird fluttered up and circled above her three times before flying off.

Eldest daughter sat on her sled and rode down the hillside until she arrived at a giant choom. Straightaway she entered and glanced about her; and the first thing that met her gaze was a fat piece of roast venison. Being hungry from her journey, she made a fire, warmed herself and warmed the meat on the fire. Then she tore off pieces of fat from the meat; she tore off one piece and ate it, then tore off another and ate that too, and another until she had eaten her fill. Just as all the fat was eaten, she heard a noise behind her and a handsome young giant entered.

It was Kotura himself.

He gazed at eldest daughter and said in his booming voice:

"Where are you from, girl? What is your mission here?"

"My father sent me," replied the girl, "to be your wife."

Kotura frowned, fell silent, then sighed.

"I've brought home some meat from hunting. Set to work and cook it for me."

Eldest daughter did as he said, and when the meat was cooked, Kotura bade her divide it in two.

"You and I will eat one part," he said. "The remainder you will take to my neighbour. But heed my words well—do not go into her choom. Wait outside until the old woman emerges. Give her the meat and wait for her to return the empty dish."

Eldest daughter took the meat and went out into the dark night. The wind was howling and the blizzard raging so wildly she could hardly see a thing before her. She struggled on a little way, then came to a halt and tossed the meat into the snow. That done, she returned to Kotura with the empty dish.

The giant looked at her keenly and said:

"Have you done as I said?"

"Certainly," replied the girl.

"Then show me the dish. I wish to see what she gave you in return," he said.

Eldest daughter showed him the empty dish. Kotura was silent. He ate his share of the meat hurriedly and lay down to sleep. At first light he rose, brought some untanned deer hides into the tent and said:

"While I hunt, I want you to clean these hides and make me a coat, shoes and mittens from them. I shall try them on when I get back and judge whether you are as clever with your hands as you are with your tongue."

With those words, Kotura went off into the tundra. And eldest daughter set to work. By and by, a wizened old woman covered in snow came into the tent.

"I have something in my eye, child," she said. "Please remove it for me."

"I've no time. I'm too busy," answered eldest daughter.

The old Snow Woman said nothing, turned away and left the tent. Eldest daughter was left alone. She cleaned the hides hastily and began cutting them roughly with a knife, hurrying to get her tasks done by nightfall. Indeed, she was in such a rush that she did not even try to shape the garments properly; she was intent only on finishing her work as quickly as possible.

Late that evening, the young giant, Lord of the Winds, returned.

"Are my clothes ready?" he asked at once.

"They are," eldest daughter replied.

Kotura took the garments one by one, and ran his hands carefully over them: the hides were rough to the touch so badly were they cleaned, so poorly were they cut, so carelessly were they sewn together. And they were altogether too small for him.

At that he flew into a rage, picked up eldest daughter and flung her far, far into the dark night. She landed in a deep snowdrift and lay there unmoving until she froze to death.

And the howling of the wind became even fiercer.

Back in the Nenets camp, the old father sat in his choom and harkened to the days blown over by the northern winds. Finally, in deep despair, he said to his two remaining daughters:

"Eldest daughter did not heed my words, I fear. That is why the wind is still shrieking and roaring its anger. Kotura is in a terrible temper. You must go to him, second daughter."

The old man made a sled, instructed the girl as he had her sister, and sent her on her way. Second daughter pointed the sled into the north wind and, giving it a push, walked along behind it. The strings of her coat came undone and the snow forced its way into her shoes. Soon she was numb with cold and, heedless of her father's warning, she shook the snow from her shoes and tied the strings of her coat sooner than she was instructed.

She came to the steep hill and climbed to the top. There, seeing the little bird fluttering towards her, she waved her hands and shooed him away. Then quickly she climbed into her sled and rode down the hillside, straight to Kotura's choom. She entered the tent, made a fire, ate her fill of the roast venison and lay down to sleep.

When Kotura returned, he was surprised to find the girl asleep on his bed. The roar of his deep voice woke her at once and she explained that her father had sent her to be his wife.

Kotura frowned, fell silent, then shouted at her gruffly:

"Then why do you lie there sleeping? I am hungry, be quick and prepare some meat."

As soon as the meat was ready, Kotura ordered second daughter to take it from the pot and cut it in half.

"You and I will eat one half," he said. "And you will take the other to my neighbour. But do not enter her choom—wait outside for the dish to be returned."

Second daughter took the meat and went outside into the storm. The wind was howling so hard, the black night was so smothering that she could see and hear nothing at all. So, fearing to take another step, she tossed the meat as far as she could and returned to Kotura's tent.

"Have you given the meat to my neighbour?" he asked.

"Of course I have," replied second daughter.

"You haven't been long," he said. "Show me the dish, I want to see what she gave you in return."

Somewhat afraid, second daughter did as she was bid, and Kotura frowned as he saw the empty dish. But he said not a word and went to bed. In the morning, he brought in some untanned hides and told second daughter to make him a coat, shoes and mittens by nightfall.

"Set to work," he said. "This evening I shall judge your handiwork."

With those words, Kotura went off into the wind and second daughter got down to her task. She was in a great hurry, eager to complete the job by nightfall. By and by, a wizened old woman covered in snow came into the tent.

"I've something in my eye, child," she said. "Pray help me take it out; I cannot manage by myself."

"Oh, go away and don't bother me," said the girl, crossly. "I am too busy to leave my work."

The Snow Woman went away without a word.

As darkness came, Kotura returned from hunting.

"Are my new clothes ready?" he asked.

"Here they are," replied second daughter.

He tried on the garments and saw at once they were poorly cut and much too small. Flying into a rage, he flung second daughter even farther than her sister. And she too met a cold death in the snow.

Back home the old father sat in the choom with his youngest daughter, waiting in vain for the storm to abate.

But the blizzard redoubled its force, and it seemed the camp would be blown away at any minute.

"My daughters did not heed my words," the old man reflected, sadly. "They have angered Kotura even more. Go to him, my last daughter, though it breaks my heart to part with you; but you alone can save our clan from certain doom."

Youngest daughter left the camp, turned her face into the north wind and pushed the sled before her. The wind shrieked and seethed about her; the snowflakes powdered her red-rimmed eyes, almost blinding her. Yet she staggered on through the blizzard, mindful of her father's words. The strings of her coat came undone—but she did not stop to tie them. The snow forced its way into her shoes—but she did not stop to shake it out. And although her face was numb and her lungs were bursting, she did not pause for breath. Only when she had reached the hilltop did she halt to shake out the snow from her shoes and tie the strings of her coat.

Just at that moment, a little bird flew down and perched on her shoulder. Instead of chasing him away, she gently stroked his downy breast.

And when the bird flew off, she got on to her sled and glided over the snow down the hillside, right to Kotura's door.

Without showing her fear, the young girl went boldly into the tent and sat down, patiently waiting for the giant to appear. It was not long before the doorflap was lifted and in came the handsome young giant, Lord of the Winds.

When he set eyes on the young girl, a smile lit up his solemn face.

"Why have you come to me?" he asked.

"My father sent me to ask you to calm the storm," she said, quietly. "For if you do not, our people will die."

Kotura frowned and said gruffly:

"Make up the fire and cook some meat. I am hungry and so must you be too, for I see you have touched nothing since you arrived."

Youngest daughter prepared the meat, took it from the pot and handed it to Kotura in a dish. But he instructed her to take half to his neighbour.

Obediently, youngest daughter took the dish of meat and went outside into the snowstorm. Where was she to go? Where was the neighbour's choom to be found in this wilderness?

Then suddenly, from out of nowhere, a little bird flew before her face—that self-same bird she had caressed on the hillside. Now it flew before her, as if beckoning her on. Whichever way the bird flew, there she followed. At last she could make out a wisp of smoke spiralling upwards and mingling with the swirling snowflakes.

Youngest daughter was very relieved, and she made for the smoke, thinking the choom must be there. Yet as she drew near, she saw to her surprise that the smoke was coming from a mound of snow; no choom was to be seen!

She walked round and round the mound of snow and prodded it with her foot. Straightaway a door appeared before her and an old, old woman poked her head out.

"Who are you?" she screeched. "And why have you come here?"

"I have brought you some meat, Grannie," youngest daughter replied. "Kotura asked me to bring it to you."

"Kotura, you say?" said the Snow Woman, chewing on a black pipe. "Very well then, wait here."

Youngest daughter waited by the strange snow-house, and at last the old woman reappeared and handed her back the wooden dish. There was something in the dish but the girl could not make it out in the dark. With a word of thanks, she took the dish and returned to Kotura.

"Why were you so long?" Kotura asked. "Did you find the Snow Woman's choom?"

"Yes, I did, but it was a long way," she replied.

"Give me the dish, that I might see what she has given you," said the giant.

When he looked into the dish he saw that it contained two sharp knives and some bone needles and scrapers for dressing hides.

The giant chuckled.

"You have some fine gifts to keep you busy."

At dawn Kotura rose and brought some deerskins into the choom. As before, he gave orders that new shoes, mittens and a coat were to be made by nightfall.

"Should you make them well," he said, "you shall be my wife."

As soon as Kotura had gone, youngest daughter set to work. The Snow Woman's gifts indeed proved very useful: there was all she needed to make the garments.

But how could she do it in single day? That was impossible!

All the same, she dressed and scraped the skins, cut and sewed so quickly that her fingers were soon raw and bleeding.

As she was about her work, the doorflap was raised and in came the old Snow Woman.

"Help me, my child," she said. "There's a mote in my eye. Pray help me to take it out."

At once youngest daughter set aside her work and soon had the mote out of the old woman's eye.

"That's better," said the Snow Woman. "My eye does not hurt any more. Now, child, look into my right ear and see what you can see."

Youngest daughter looked into the old woman's right ear and gasped in surprise.

"What do you see?" the Snow Woman asked.

"I see a maid sitting in your ear," the girl replied.

"Then, why don't you call to her? She will help you make Kotura's clothes."

At her call, not one but four maids jumped from the Snow Woman's ear and immediately set to work. They dressed the skins, scraped them smooth, cut and sewed them into shape, and very soon the garments were all ready. Then the Snow Woman took the four maids back into her ear and left the choom.

As darkness fell, Kotura returned.

"Have you completed your tasks?" he asked.

"Yes, I have," the girl said.

"Then show me the new clothes, that I may try them on."

Youngest daughter handed him the clothes, and Kotura passed his great hand over them: the skins were soft and supple to the touch. He put them on: the coat and the shoes and the mittens. And they were neither small nor large. They fitted him perfectly.

Kotura smiled.

"I like you, youngest daughter," he said. "And my mother and four sisters like you, too. You work well, and you have much courage. You braved a terrible storm so that your people might not die. And you did all that you were told. Stay with me and be my wife."

No sooner had the words passed his lips than the storm in the tundra was stilled. No longer did the Nenets people hide from the north wind in their cold tents. They were saved. One by one they emerged into the sunshine.

And with them came the old father, tears of joy glistening on his sunken cheeks, proud that his youngest, dearest daughter had saved the people from the storm.

I love this story, although it is one of those tales that praises a girl for doing as she is told. The Snow Woman and the four daughters in her ear—what a wonderful image! And the heroine doesn't just win the heart of the Lord of the Winds by being obedient. She also wins it because she's compassionate and doesn't put herself first. She is courageous and able to fight her fear.

How would this tale pan out, I wondered while rereading it, if the father had had three sons instead of daughters? It would be an interesting task to rewrite all fairy tales in that manner: exchanging daughters for sons and vice versa. In this tale, the father certainly wouldn't have sent his sons off to become the willing husbands of the Queen of the Winds. No, he'd probably have given them the task of fighting her. And the youngest one, considered a fool or a weakling, would have killed the queen and saved the world with this act of destruction. In contrast, the tasks the daughters are told to perform are typical women's tasks: bringing food to an old neighbour, sewing clothes... What if the Lord of the Winds said, "Girl, prove to me you're the right wife for me by fighting that mean bear who growls in front of my house every night"? *What if he said,* "Let's have a race on my storm horses, and if you win I'll make you my wife"?*

Yes, what if one day tales are told in such a way that men and women may finally—or once again?—be equals?

Through
the Water
Curtain

A wandering monk came to the province of Hida where, deep in the mountains, he got lost. Following a faint track buried in dead leaves, he finally came to a wide, high waterfall that cascaded like a great curtain down a cliff. He could not go back since he had no idea where he was, and in front of him rose a two-hundred-foot wall of rock. While praying to the Buddha for guidance, he heard footsteps behind him. It was a man with a load of wood. Though the monk was relieved to see him, the man looked surprised and upset. "Who are you? Where does this path go?" asked the monk, but the man walked straight past him into the waterfall and vanished.

Apparently he had been a demon, not a man. The frightened monk decided that before the demon ate him, he would plunge into the waterfall too, and die. "Then it won't bother me if he does eat me!" he said to himself.

Praying for a happy rebirth, he walked straight ahead till water pounded on his face. Then he was through.

He supposed drowning came next, but in fact he still seemed to be conscious. The waterfall really *was* a thin curtain, and the narrow path on the other side led on under the mountain. He was glad at last to reach a large village.

The man who had passed him now came running towards him, ahead of a gentleman in light blue-green formal dress. The gentleman hastily invited the monk to follow him home. On the way, people joined them from all directions and each one asked the monk home. What could they all want? The gentleman silenced them. "We'll go to the mayor and let him decide who gets this fellow!" he said.

The crowd swept the monk on to a large house, where an agitated old man came out and asked what was going on. The first man the monk had seen complained, "I'm the one who led him here from Japan, and now this man has taken him over!" He pointed at the gentleman in blue-green.

Without discussion the old man awarded the monk to the gentleman, who began leading the monk away. The crowd dispersed.

The monk could only think they were all demons, and that this one was taking him away to eat him. He began to cry. "Japan!" he thought in despair. "Where *is* this place if Japan is so far away?"

The gentleman noticed his expression. "Please don't worry!" he said. "It's very peaceful here, you know. I promise you you'll be comfortable. You won't have a care in the world."

The gentleman's house turned out to be a little smaller than the one they had just left, but very nice and with a large staff of servants and retainers. The monk's arrival caused a great stir. When the gentleman invited him in, his pack, straw cloak, hat and straw boots were politely taken from him and put away.

"Food, please!" the gentleman ordered, and a meal was served. But despite the wealth of beautifully prepared chicken and fish, the monk did not eat. Instead he only sat and stared.

His host asked him what was the matter.

"I've been a monk all my life, you see, and I've never eaten anything like this. Looking is all I can do."

"I understand. But you're with *us* now, you know. You'll have to eat up! And another thing. I have a daughter I love very much and she's ready to be married. So you should start letting your hair grow, because I want her to marry *you*. You can't leave, anyway. Just remember to do as I say!"

The monk thought he might be killed if he showed any sign of resistance, and there certainly was no escape. "I'm just not used to this sort of food," he answered, "but all right, I'll eat it." As the two ate, the monk wondered what the Buddha could be thinking of him now, since he had vowed never to eat the flesh of any living creature.

At nightfall a very pretty girl came in, beautifully dressed. Her father pushed her gently towards the monk. "She's yours," he said. "From now on you must love her as much as I do. She's my only daughter, you understand, so you can imagine how deeply I mean that." With this little speech he withdrew.

No argument was possible. The monk (from now on he will have to be "the young man") welcomed the girl, and after that they were man and wife. The young man was actually very happy. He was dressed in the best and served whatever food he wanted. This new life was so unlike his old one that he put on a good deal of weight. When his hair was long enough for a topknot he did it up properly, and with a respectable hat on he cut a fine figure. His wife thought the world of him and he loved her in return.

After eight months like this, the young woman grew sad. Her father, on the other hand, only redoubled his attentions. "Good, good, we've gotten some flesh on you!" he would say. "Fatten up all you like!" He fed his son-in-law so often that the young man kept putting on weight. As he did so, his wife began to have fits of weeping. When the young man asked her why, she would answer only that she felt sad, but wept more and more. The baffled young man put up with it as best he could.

One day his father-in-law entertained a visitor. Listening in discreetly, he heard the visitor say, "That's a nice young man you've got! You must be pleased to have your daughter so well provided for."

"I certainly am!" the gentleman answered. "If I didn't have him, I don't know how I could stand it by now."

"I just wish I could get one myself," said the visitor, rising to go. "I'm sure I'll be miserable by this time next year."

Having seen his guest off, the gentleman asked solicitously whether his son-in-law had eaten, and made sure a meal was served. The young man's wife wept while he ate. The puzzled young man kept thinking about what the visitor had said, and although he did not quite understand it, he was afraid. His wife resisted every effort of his to coax an explanation out of her, though she clearly wanted to speak.

The village was bustling with preparations for a festival. Depressed as she was, the young man's wife now did little more than cry, and she seemed so estranged from him that he finally reproached her. "I thought we'd always be together in joy and sorrow," he complained, "but you've gotten so far away! You're too cruel!" He burst into angry tears.

His wife sobbed aloud. "Whatever made me think I could keep silent till the very end?" she cried. "There's so little time left! Oh, if only I didn't love you!"

"Am I going to die? Well, so are we all, some time or other. There must be something else! Tell me!"

"You see, we have a sacred obligation here to give our gods living human sacrifices. That's why everyone was so anxious to have you when you came. They all wanted you for the sacrifice. Each year it's another household's turn to provide the victim, and if no one from outside can be found, the household head has to provide his own son or daughter. I'd have been the victim if you hadn't come. Oh, I wish I could take your place after all!"

"Don't cry!" said her husband. "Perhaps it could be worse. Tell me, is the victim carved up *before* being offered to the gods?"

"No, I don't think so. The victim is laid out naked on a cutting board and carried inside the inner sanctuary fence. Then everyone leaves. I hear the gods carve up their victim themselves. If the victim is thin or displeasing in any way, they're very angry. Then the crops fail, people get sick, and we villagers do nothing but quarrel. That's why my father has been feeding you so often and making you gain weight."

At last the young man understood all the care that had been lavished on him. "But these gods," he said, "what shape do they have?"

"They're supposed to be monkeys."

"All right, I have an idea. Can you get me a good dagger?"

"Of course I can," his wife answered, and quickly did so.

The young man sharpened it carefully and hid it on his body. He got much livelier now, ate with unfailing appetite, and went on fattening nicely. His father-in-law was pleased, and everyone in the village looked forward to a good year.

Seven days before the festival, ceremonial ropes were stretched around all the houses to mark the sacred occasion, and the young man was made to fast and undergo purification. Though his wife counted the days with tears and groans, he himself seemed untroubled. In fact, he comforted his wife so well that even she took heart a little.

On the festival day he was made to wash and put on a beautiful robe. His hair was combed and tied up, and his sidelocks carefully dressed. A messenger came from the shrine again and again, more impatient each time. Finally the young man and the gentleman rode out on horses together while the young wife stayed behind, hiding under her robe and weeping in silence.

The shrine was a row of sanctuaries composing a single large structure inside an impressively fenced sacred enclosure. The crowd before the fence was eating a festive meal. The young man was led to a high seat among them and served food too. After the company had eaten and drunk freely, there was dancing and music.

At last the young man was called on to rise. He was undressed, his hair was unbound, and he was laid on the cutting board with a final, strict order neither to move nor to speak. Green sprigs of the sacred *sakaki* tree were planted at the board's four corners, and a sacred cord with white streamers fluttering from it was strung from sprig to sprig. Having carried the board ceremoniously through the fence and laid it before the sanctuaries, the bearers withdrew and closed the gate behind them. The young man was all alone. He stealthily reached for the dagger hidden all this time between his thighs.

When the door of the chief sanctuary creaked open, the young man's hair stood on end. One by one the other doors opened too. Next a monkey as big as a man came round from behind the shrine and chattered at the chief sanctuary. The sanctuary curtain was swept aside and out came another monkey with gleaming white teeth, larger and fiercer than the first. "They're just monkeys after all!" thought the young man with relief. More monkeys came from the other sanctuaries, and when all were present the messenger monkey received chattered orders from the monkey of the chief sanctuary. These instructions obviously concerned the victim because the messenger monkey now came to the cutting board, picked up the large cooking chopsticks and knife that were laid out for him, and prepared to carve.

The young man leapt up and attacked the chief monkey who, taken completely by surprise, toppled over backwards. A dagger pinned him to the ground. "Are you a god?" the young man roared. The monkey wrung his hands beseechingly while all the others fled and sat chattering furiously in the treetops.

The young man tied up the monkey with some vines that came to hand and bound him to a post. Then, with his dagger to the pit of the monkey's stomach, he cried, "Why, you *are* just a plain monkey! And all these years you've been calling yourself a god and eating people! *Now* what have you got to say for yourself? All right, call out your sons! Call them out! You're dead if you don't. Of course, if you're a god my knife won't hurt you. Perhaps I'll just stick it in your belly and see what happens!" A little pressure on the blade made the monkey scream and wring his hands again. "All right," said the young man, "call out your sons!"

The monkey chattered and the messenger monkey came back. Sending him for more vines, the young man first tied up the chief monkey's three sons, then the messenger monkey too. "You were going to carve me up," he said, "but I'll let you live if you stay quiet. I will kill you, though, if you ever curse those poor, ignorant people again or eat them!"

He led the monkeys out the gate through the shrine fence and tied them to trees. Next, he set fire to the shrine with embers from the recent cooking fires. The village was so far off that no one knew, though when flames leapt from the spot, the villagers saw them and worried. No one went to see what was happening because people were supposed to stay at home for three days after the festival.

The gentleman was particularly upset and feared something had gone very wrong. His daughter too was afraid because she knew better than her father what might have caused the flames. Then the victim himself appeared in the village, carrying a staff and driving the tied-up monkeys ahead of him. He was naked but for a belt of vines with a dagger stuck in it, and his loose hair flowed over his shoulders. People peeped at him through every gate along the way. "He's got the gods bound and he's driving them along!" they cried to each other. "Why, our sacrificial victim was more powerful than the gods! And if he can do this to the gods, just think what he can do to *us*! Maybe he'll eat us!" The villagers were terrified.

At his father-in-law's house the young man shouted for the gate to be opened. Silence met his demand. "Open up!" he shouted again. "I won't hurt you! But if you don't open up there *will* be trouble." He kicked at the gate.

The gentleman had his daughter go out to meet her husband. "He's stronger than the gods," he said, "and I'm afraid he may mean you harm. But open the gate and talk to him."

Fearful but happy too, the girl cracked the gate open and the young man pushed it wide. "Let me have my clothes," he said. She fetched him his trousers, his cloak and his hat, and after tying the monkeys fast to the house he dressed. He also had her bring him a quiver and bow. Then he called out his father-in-law.

"It's horrible!" he said. "These are *monkeys* you've been calling gods and feeding people to all these years. Look! This is Mr. Monkey. You can keep him tied to your house, and if anyone does any tormenting it's *you*, not Mr. Monkey. But you've had it all backwards! Well, you can be sure these monkeys won't trouble you any more as long as I'm here!"

He pinched one of the monkeys' ears. It did not react. The whole thing was rather funny. The monkeys seemed quite tame! Slightly reassured, the gentleman agreed that they had had everything wrong. "From now on *you'll* be our god," he said, "and we'll do whatever you say!" He rubbed his hands together ingratiatingly.

The young man led him off to see the mayor, herding the monkeys along. His knock on the gate again got no answer.

"Open up!" the gentleman shouted. "I've got to speak to you! There'll be trouble otherwise!" This threat brought out the mayor, trembling with fear, to open up. At the sight of the sacrificial victim he threw himself prostrate on the ground. The young man led his monkeys into the house and spoke to them with fury in his eyes. "You've falsely called yourselves gods, and each year you've killed and eaten a human being. Now you're going to mend your ways!" He fitted an arrow to his bowstring and took aim. The monkeys screamed in abject fear, and the mayor was so alarmed that he asked the gentleman, "Is he going to kill us, too? Save us!"

"Keep calm," the gentleman answered. "Nothing will happen as long as I'm here."

"All right," the young man went on, "I won't have your lives. But if you ever show yourselves here again, and try any mischief against the people, I promise I'll shoot you."

He gave each monkey twenty blows of his staff, then sent the villagers to smash and burn what was left of the shrine. Next, he drove the monkeys out of the village. They ran off, limping, deep into the mountains and were never seen again.

Now the greatest man in the village, the young man stayed on with his wife. The villagers were at his beck and call. Perhaps he told this story when he came back to our land for a secret visit. Since the people beyond the waterfall had no cattle, horses or dogs, he brought them puppies (dogs are great enemies of monkeys) and foals for them to put to work, and these all multiplied. But although he sometimes visited our land, no one from here ever visited his.

Is there any Western fairy tale that begins with a monk? Our Western tales tend to be quite worldly. At the end the hero has plenty of gold and a crown and the most beautiful girl—a happy ending that makes one wonder whether our civilization always defined success in material gain and the fulfilment of all desires.

In Asian tales, the king often gives away all his wealth and becomes a hermit in a cave in the end. Success is defined as overcoming desire.

This tale from Japan is somehow between those two beliefs. The hero is a monk, but he soon becomes a married man and saves his wife and her whole village from superstition and false gods. The central theme of this story, human sacrifice, can be found in many Western tales, but we're mostly used to dragons claiming virgins as regular sacrifices, until a knight comes by to slay them. The monk-turned-happily-married-man is more to my taste. He reminds me of the hero in The Story of One Who Set Out to Study Fear. *I like that he doesn't slay the treacherous monkeys and—surprise!—he doesn't return to our world but stays in the land he found behind the waterfall. Fairy tales often punish their heroes for staying in otherworldly realms. Not this one. He is allowed to go back and forth and to enjoy without regret the hidden land he discovered, for this is a light-hearted tale. Even human sacrifice seems like a minor unpleasantness, and surely there is nothing to be found behind the water curtain that resembles the darkness of a Bluebeard or a gingerbread house.*

The
Areca
Tree

an and Lang were brothers. Though Tan was a year older than Lang, they were as alike in looks as two drops of water. No one could tell them apart. No one, that is, except the lovely Thao, whose father taught the village youth. During their years of studies together, Tan, Lang and Thao became the best of friends.

At first, Thao could not distinguish between the two brothers. They wore identical clothes and their hair was cut the same way. Then one stormy night when the brothers stayed late at their teacher's home, Thao saw her chance. She prepared rice porridge for their meal and brought out one bowl and one pair of chopsticks and placed them on the table between the two brothers. She returned to the kitchen and watched them through a crack in the door. One brother motioned to the other to eat first, a privilege reserved for an elder brother. Now Thao knew which brother was Tan. She quickly brought out a second bowl for Lang. All evening, she observed the brothers carefully, until she managed to discover one small difference between them. Lang had a tiny mole on his right ear.

After that, her father and classmates were impressed by Thao's ability to tell the brothers apart. She never handed Tan's notebook to Lang, and she always greeted each brother by his own name. Over time, Thao noticed differences in the brothers' personalities. Tan was outgoing and talkative. Lang tended to be quiet and pensive. Gradually, she could tell them apart merely by looking into their eyes. And although their voices were similar, she was sensitive enough to hear each boy's nature expressed in his words.

One New Year's Day, the two brothers came to offer their respects to Thao's father. Suddenly Thao realized that Tan was in love with her. She couldn't explain exactly why, but the look in his eyes let her know beyond the shadow of a doubt. And as for Lang? Thao was so shaken by Tan's look, she did not notice Lang's.

Not long afterwards, Tan's parents brought the traditional offering of salt to Thao's parents to ask for her hand in marriage to their elder son. Thao's parents agreed. With some regret, Thao left the home of her parents to go live with her husband's family. She wished that her people still followed the old custom of having the groom live with the bride's family. But she loved Tan and was happy to be his wife. On their wedding day,

Tan wore a robe the cheerful colour of green banana shoots. Lang's robe was a deep shade of violet.

Each day, Thao saw how deeply her husband loved his younger brother. When she and Tan strolled beneath the moonlight, drank tea, went horseback riding or played chess, Tan always invited Lang to join them. In fact, Lang wanted the couple to enjoy time alone, but Tan insisted on Lang's presence. Lang pretended to enjoy these occasions, while deep down he longed for more solitude. He found great contentment spending quiet moments on his own. Tan was unable to understand this need in his brother and could not bear the thought of Lang being left alone. Thao tried to speak to Tan about Lang's special needs, but Tan would not listen.

A new discovery added to Thao's concern. Lang was also in love with her. Love burnt within him like a fiery volcano. Although he appeared cool and indifferent on the outside, Thao was sensitive enough to know the truth.

One day Lang told them he wanted to retire to a remote mountain hut where he could tend a garden and compose poems. Thao hoped her husband would support Lang's idea, but instead he insisted Lang remain with them.

One dark evening, when the brothers returned from a day's labour in the rice fields, Thao mistook Lang for her husband when he entered their hut first. She opened her arms to greet him. Lang hastily removed himself from her embrace and Thao realized her error.

The next morning as they shared rice porridge, Lang informed Tan and Thao that he was taking the day off. Though he laughed as he spoke, Thao detected his anguish. She loved her husband, but that did not prevent her from feeling Lang's pain.

Lang did not return that evening. Ten days passed and there was still no word from him. Frantic, Tan left home to search for his brother. Ten more days passed and neither brother had returned. Thao was beside herself with worry. She left home herself to look for Tan. Like both brothers, she followed the road that led out of the capital city's southern gate. There the road forked. One side led up into the mountains, the other down to the sea. She chose the mountain route.

Thao walked for days until her sandals were no more than shreds and her feet were swollen and bloody. Matted locks of hair fell into her eyes. All she had left was a straw hat to protect her from the sun. She felt almost too weak to continue. Her heart was filled with dread.

Somehow she knew that Tan and Lang had passed by this same way, and that knowledge alone kept her going. She tore strips of cloth from her shirt to wrap her blistered feet and trudged on until she came to the banks of a wide river. It was evening, and there was no ferry in sight. A slight wind rustled overhead leaves, and a few birds called in shrill voices. Thao was prepared to spend the night by the river, when she noticed a tiny hut perched on stilts a couple of hundred yards away on her side of the shore. A sudden gust of wind sent dry leaves flying. Black clouds gathered at the horizon. Thao knew a storm was brewing. She made her way to the hut and climbed up the ladder to knock on the door. She was greeted, somewhat cautiously, by a woman who looked at her oddly but then urged her to enter. She took Thao's hat and invited her to be seated on a low bamboo bench. Dinner was spread out on a simple mat. Thao greeted the woman's husband, who was feeding their baby spoonfuls of rice.

The woman took out an extra bowl and chopsticks for Thao but Thao politely declined. She was too exhausted to eat but gladly accepted a bowl of hot tea. There was a sudden crash of thunder outside. Wind howled and rain beat against the hut. The sounds of the storm momentarily quieted the storm raging in Thao's own heart. The highland farmer lit a small lamp, which cast a dim light. His wife put their child to bed in the next room, the strains of her lullaby drowned out by the raging storm.

When the baby was asleep, the woman rejoined them. Thao asked the couple, "Have you, by any chance, seen a young man in a green robe pass by this way recently?"

Neither the man nor his wife spoke. The man looked at Thao with a strange expression.

Frightened, Thao asked, "Has something happened? Have you seen him then?"

The man slowly answered, "Yes, we did see such a man. What's more, we saw another man who looked just like him but was dressed in white. But I don't think you'll be finding either of them now. Please spend the night with us. You can't go out again in this storm. Tomorrow you can return safely home."

A chill ran down Thao's spine. A feeling of doom closed in around her, as she listened to the woman speak. "Move in a little closer so you can escape the draft that sneaks in by the door. I'll tell you everything we know.

"One afternoon, about a month ago, I saw a man dressed in white approach the river. He was empty-handed and didn't have even a hat or jacket. My husband was still working in the fields. I wanted to run out and tell the man that he had just missed the last ferry of the day, but I was occupied with the baby and couldn't go out right then. The man looked as if he was searching for something. It was odd, Miss, how he looked up at the sky and down at the ground. He turned his head this way and that before sitting down on the riverbank and holding his face in his hands. He began to shake and I could tell he was weeping. I felt uneasy and wanted my husband to hurry home so he could invite the poor fellow up to our hut. It began to rain lightly, and the man raised his head to the sky again. Then I thought he saw something, because he stretched out his arms as if to embrace someone. But, Miss, all he embraced was the empty air. The rain started coming down harder and soon I could not make him out very clearly. When my husband returned from the fields, I handed him a rain jacket and asked him to go down and fetch the fellow."

The highland farmer took a long sip of tea and said, "I found him sitting like a stone down by the riverbank, not flinching a muscle in all that wind and rain. I asked him several times to put on the jacket and join us inside, but he only shook his head. Finally, I left the jacket on the ground beside him and returned alone. The rain was really pouring by then."

"It was a storm like tonight," said the woman. "We couldn't fall asleep thinking about that poor fellow. All we could hope was that he'd get up out of the rain and return to his home. At dawn, all that was left of the storm was a light drizzle. I looked out the door and thought I saw the man still sitting by the riverbank. I put on a jacket and made my way out. Imagine my surprise when I realized it wasn't the man at all but a large white rock. Next to the rock was the rain jacket my husband had left the night before."

The man spoke, "It was so strange, Miss. That pure white rock hadn't ever been there before. We don't see any rocks like that up in these parts. It seemed unlikely that the man had dragged it there in the night. Anyway, I don't think four men could have budged a stone that size. Rocks don't just spring up out of the earth overnight. We couldn't figure it out. As for the man, we guessed he'd returned the way he'd come or perhaps even thrown himself into the river. That's what my wife thought, anyway, but I couldn't imagine what would drive a man to such desperate measures."

The farmer lit his pipe and took a long, thoughtful puff. His wife continued, "Ten days later another man, dressed in green, came. He looked all around him, too, like he was lost. Then he came up to our house and asked if we'd seen the other man dressed in white. When my husband told him all we'd seen, his eyes filled with tears. He cried out, 'My brother has turned to stone!' He ran to the river to find the rock just as it was beginning to rain. We had another storm and, though we tried to convince the man to come inside, he refused to budge from the rock. He leant against it and wept bitterly. Once again, my husband and I spent a sleepless night. In the morning, when we went outside, we didn't see the man, but there was a tree of the palm family, tall as a ten-year-old child, growing beside the rock. That tree hadn't been there before. What kind of tree grows that fast? I told my husband that the man dressed in green must have turned into the tree and that the rock was the man dressed in white. I believe the two men were brothers who loved each other deeply. Some terrible sorrow or misunderstanding must have taken place between them. But you, Miss, are you related to those men? Why are you looking for them? It's another stormy night. Please don't think of going out again. Stay with us tonight, I implore you."

Thao wiped tears from her eyes and made an effort to smile. To ease the mountain couple, she pretended to make light of the whole affair, "Don't worry about me. I'm the housekeeper of the man dressed in green. The man dressed in white is my master's younger brother. I'm sure they simply crossed the river early in the morning after the storms. I'll be crossing the river tomorrow myself. I'm sure I'll find them. I doubt they've gone too far. Please don't worry—I have no intention of venturing out in this storm tonight. I'd be grateful to spend the night here and then I'll catch the first ferry in the morning."

Having reassured them, Thao asked for a mat to serve as a blanket and, after the couple retired to the back room, she lay down. Wind shrieked and battered at the walls as Thao's tears soaked her mat. The lamp's wick cast a bare flicker of light that trembled in the cold drafts seeping in through the doorway. A deafening clap of thunder made Thao wonder if heaven and earth had been reduced to dust.

The storm's fury seemed endless. But at long last, the winds died down. Shortly before dawn, all was quiet. Thao rose, careful not to make a sound. She opened the door and climbed down the ladder. A bright moon emerged from wisps of cloud. By its light, Thao could easily make out the white rock by the shore. Slowly she walked towards it.

It was just as the kind couple had described. A tree with bright green leaves and trunk stood by the rock, slightly bending over as if to protect it. Thao knelt by the rock and put her arms around the tree. She hid her face in its leaves and wept. Some of her warm tears fell on the rock and seemed to sizzle. Clinging to the tree, her knees sank into the soft, muddy earth.

When the couple awoke, the young woman was gone. They went down to shore and asked the ferryman if he had carried her across the river. He replied, "No, this is my first trip of the day. I haven't carried anyone across yet."

They asked if days before he had carried a man dressed in green or a man dressed in white. Again the answer was no. The couple walked to the white rock. The tree had grown a good two feet in the night and clinging to it was a fresh, green vine. The roots of the vine began deep beneath the rock which it stretched across before twining gracefully up the tree. It almost seemed to be supporting the tree to stand upright. They plucked a vine leaf and crumbled it. It gave an ardent fragrance which reminded them of the young woman whose gaze had been so deep the night before.

*

One summer afternoon, a party on horseback, led by King Hung Vuong II, came to rest along the riverbank. They noticed a small shrine sheltered beneath several large trees. King Hung dismounted close to the shrine. There he sat down on a smooth white rock while fanning himself. An attendant offered to wave the fan for him, but the king shook his head and smiled. He pointed to the tall, straight trees around them and asked the attendant, "What kind of trees are these? The upper branches are laden with fruit. And do you know whose shrine this is?"

The attendant did not know, but seeing the king's curiosity, he climbed one of the trees and picked two of the fruits. Another attendant standing nearby said,

"Your majesty, I do not know the name of these trees or fruit, but I do know something about their origin and why the shrine is here."

He told the king the story of Tan, Lang and Thao as he had once heard it in detail from the mountain couple.

"Your majesty, the white rock you are sitting on is the kind of rock Lang turned into. The fruit in your hand comes from the kind of tree Tan turned into. And the green vines that you see twining around the trees are like the vine Thao became. People in these parts say that the white rock represents Lang's pure heart. The tall, straight trees that shade the rocks represent Tan's desire to protect his younger brother, and the graceful vine shows the spirit of Thao, who even after death remains at her husband's side. When the parents of these young people came looking for them, the farmer and his wife explained what had happened. The two families had this shrine built. Since then, local people have continued to light incense here to honour the memory of Tan, Lang and Thao."

King Hung regarded the fruit in his hand for a long moment. He looked at the trees and vines and gently patted the white rock as though it were a small child. He was deeply moved by the story. He handed the fruit to his attendant and said, "Please cut this fruit so I might taste it."

The attendant took out a knife, peeled the fruit, and cut it into eight sections. Each slice of the white fruit held a portion of a smooth pink seed. The king placed a slice in his mouth. It was not sweet like a guava but had a special tang he found refreshing. He crumbled a vine leaf and chewed it along with the fruit. The combined taste was even better. His mouth watered and he spat. A few drops of his saliva fell on the white rock and turned as red as blood. The king put a finger in his mouth and pulled it out but there was no trace of red on it. He asked his attendant to scrape off a small chip of rock which he chewed with the fruit and leaf. His lips were soon stained as red as a young maiden's.

He invited his companions to taste a bit of fruit with leaf and rock. They all found the tangy taste most agreeable, and soon their lips were stained red, as well.

King Hung spoke, "The love and bond between two brothers and husband and wife has borne a deep and ardent fruit. I decree that from now on this fruit and leaf and rock will be used in place of the traditional offering of salt for marriage proposals and weddings. They shall be symbols of love and fidelity."

The others bowed to acknowledge the king's decree. Soon after that the trees and vines were planted throughout the kingdom. The trees were named "Cao" after Tan and Lang's family name, and the vine was called "Lu" after Thao's family name. Thus the custom of chewing areca wrapped in a betel leaf with a sliver of quicklime began among the people.

There are many tales about people turning into trees, in all parts of the world. Most of the time the reason is love—maybe because the branches reaching for the sky are such a perfect symbol for the yearning love can bring. And don't these tales make us realize how much the slender silhouette of a tree resembles the human body? Yes. I think from time to time we all wish for the roots of a tree.

The
Maid of the
Copper
Mountain

One summer day, two men were on their way home from the mine. Both earned their living digging rock and clay in search of copper nuggets and precious stones, especially the bright-green malachite and rose-red rubies.

One was young, still single, but already pale and haggard from the hard work in the mine. The other was older, a sad husk of a man, his eyes sunken and cheeks flushed; when he coughed, as he did often, his whole body shook.

Their hearts felt light as they walked through the forest; the finches were chirping gaily, the earth smelled good, of moist moss, and the air, freshened by recent rain, was heady with the scent of pines and firs. With the long walk and warm day, the men were soon tired, and they rested on the grass beneath a cherry tree. It was not long before both fell asleep.

Suddenly, the younger man woke with a start. He rubbed his eyes and there, sitting on a moss-green rock, was a young maiden. She had her back to him and had not noticed the two slumbering men. Her long plait was as black as a raven's wing. It did not swing freely like most girls' do, but lay straight and tidy, as if fixed to her back. Its reddish-green ribbons glistened and softly rustled like slender copper leaves.

The lad stared at the plait and then gazed fondly at the girl. She would not keep still for a moment, bobbing up and down like dandelion fluff in a gusty wind. One moment she would stoop to search beneath her feet, the next she would bob up again, then twist and turn to left and right. She would leap up, arms outstretched, then sit quite still. Like a piece of quicksilver! And all the time she chattered away in some strange tongue—with whom, he could not tell. From the merry ring of her voice, she was evidently enjoying herself.

The young man dearly wished to utter a word, yet he feared she would take fright and run away. All of a sudden a fearful thought struck him: "My, this must be the Malachite Maid herself. That's her robe all right. And her jet-black hair."

Her robe was truly wonderful. Folk say it was woven into silk from malachite stone and the collar trimmed with golden lace.

"Now I'm in trouble," thought the lad. "Perhaps I can creep away without her seeing me."

The elders of the village had told how the Malachite Maid could turn men to pillars of stone for just looking at her.

Scarcely had the thought entered his head than the girl turned. Her lips parted in a smile as she beckoned him closer.

"Now there's a fine thing, Stepanushko. You can't gaze at a maid's charms for nothing, you know. You must pay for your boldness. Come here. You and I must have a talk."

The young man was afraid, but he tried to hide it: she was only a girl after all—though a bewitched one.

"I've no time to stop and gossip," he said. "I've overslept as it is. We have to be home by sundown."

She only laughed at him. "Do as I command. I want a word with you."

He made his way forward, thinking it best to please her. Yet as he rounded her rock, he found himself amidst an army of lizards, all different: some were green, some the shades of blue, others the colour of sand or clay speckled with gold, some shone like glass or mica, some were dull like parched grass, and others were criss-crossed and zigzagged by all sorts of patterns.

The girl just sat there smiling.

"Don't you step on my troops, Stepanushko. You are so big and clumsy, and my soldiers are so tiny."

Then she clapped her hands; the lizards scuttled aside and left a path clear.

He stepped forward carefully and, once he had reached her, she again clapped her hands.

"Now there's nowhere you can tread," she said mockingly. "If you crush any of my servants, I'll turn you into a lizard."

He looked down at his feet, but could not see the ground for lizards, lizards and more lizards. All the lizards had clustered together—like a patchwork quilt around his feet. He blinked and rubbed his eyes, and when he looked again—the lizards had turned to copper crystals. All sorts and finely polished. And among them nestled gold, and pale-blue sapphires, green malachite and wine-red rubies.

"Now do you recognize me, my bold Stepanushko?" asked the Malachite Maid, and a gay laugh dimpled her sunny cheeks. "But don't be afraid. I shall do you no harm."

Stepan blushed. No girl had ever made fun of him like that, nor talked to him so boldly. He became quite cross, even shouted at her.

"You can't scare me. I'm used to toiling in the mine; even the master holds no fear for me."

"That's the spirit," replied the maid. "I need a fearless fellow like you. Listen carefully to what I say. Tomorrow, when you go to the mine, your master will be there. Tell him this, and mind you forget not a word: 'The Maid of the Copper Mountain,' you must say, 'has ordered you, you stinking goat, to clear out of the mine. If your hammers dent her copper crown, she'll bury all the copper so deep you'll never find it again.'"

She gazed at Stepan long and hard.

"Will you remember my words, Stepanushko? You toil in the mine, you say, and fear no one. So just you tell your master that to his face. Now off you go; say nothing to your friend. The poor man has enough ill fortune of his own. I've told one of my lizards to slip a small gift into his pocket."

At that, she clapped her hands once more, scattering the lizards to all sides. Then she sprang upon the rock and scampered about on all fours, lizard-like. In place of hands and feet, she grew little green paws and a black-striped green tail. Yet she kept the lovely head of a girl, which looked down at him.

"Don't forget, Stepanushko. Tell your master the Malachite Maid says he's a stinking goat and he must leave the mine. Tell him that and... I'll be your wife!"

That was too much for Stepan; he spat in disgust.

"Ugh, you horrid creature. What, me—marry a lizard?!" His disgust only amused her.

"All right," she cried, "we'll see about that later. Perhaps you'll change your mind."

Thereupon, with a flick of her green tail, she vanished behind the rock.

Stepan stood alone, lost in thought. Then he gave his friend a shake, saying nothing of the girl, and they continued on their way. It was evening before they reached the village. Stepan wondered what he was to do. To say those words to his master was more than his job was worth. Yet if he held his tongue, he risked a fate no man would envy. After all, she was the Maid of the Copper Mountain: she could turn the gold he found into fool's gold, into a handful of dust. How would he make his living then? And another thing; he did not want the girl to think him an idle boaster.

He spent a troubled, sleepless night, but by morning his mind was made up: "I'll do as she says and take what comes."

Later, at the mine, when the master appeared, all the miners, as usual, bowed their heads and stood silent—everyone, that is, except Stepan. He marched straight up to him.

"I met the Maid of the Copper Mountain yesterday. She orders you to clear out of the mine, you stinking goat. And if you dent her copper crown, she says she'll bury the copper so deep you'll never find it again."

The very ends of the master's whiskers quivered with rage.

"What's that, are you drunk or plain mad? What Maid? Who do you think you're talking to? I'll have you rot in the deepest pit for this!"

"As you will," said Stepan. "I'm only saying what she told me."

"Flog him," yelled the master, "then chain him in the bottom-most pit. Toss him enough pigswill to keep him alive and if he slacks or tries any tricks, flog him without mercy!"

So poor Stepan was flogged and dragged down to the bottom-most pit. It was damp, and water dripped from the walls. There they chained him to the rock, with just enough space to swing his pick. There was nothing for it. As soon as the master had gone, Stepan began to hack at the rock and was amazed to see malachite come tumbling down—it was as if some invisible hand was tossing him lumps of the best malachite crystal. And the water drained away, the shaft became quite dry and airy.

"Well now," he thought, "it seems as if the Maid hasn't forsaken me after all."

Nor had she, for he suddenly heard his name called softly and the Maid appeared in a green glow.

"Well done, Stepan. I'm proud of you. You were not afraid of the stinking goat. You spoke up well. Come along and claim your reward. I too stand by my word."

But a frown clouded her lovely face, as if this was not to her liking. She gave a clap of her hands and the lizards came scurrying to unchain Stepan; she gave each one his orders: they were to pick and polish the best silk malachite. Then she turned to Stepan: "Come and see my wedding gift to you."

And off they went, she in front, Stepan closely following. Wherever she walked, the mountain walls opened up, and they passed into underground caverns with walls of every texture and hue: now a green satin, now velvet flecked with gold, and now a coppery grain. There were misty-blue walls too, of sapphires. It was all too wonderful to describe. And her dress constantly changed colour to match the stones: one moment it shimmered with all the colours of the rainbow, the next it glittered with diamonds, then it turned coppery red, then again a silky green. And so they went on and on. At last she stopped.

"Here we are, right at the heart of the mountain—my favourite room."

Stepan saw they were in a huge chamber, with a couch, tables and chairs—all of royal copper. The walls were of malachite studded with diamonds and the ceiling dark crimson ringed by copper flowers.

They sat down on the copper chairs and the Malachite Maid asked him, "So you have seen my wedding gift?"

"Yes, it takes my breath away," replied Stepan.

"Well, and what do you say now to having me for your wife?"

Poor Stepan did not know what to say. He already had a sweetheart, a good girl, an orphan. Of course, she did not match the Maid for looks. She was only a plain village girl. Stepan hesitated, then said finally: "Your dowry is fit for a tsar, and I'm only a working man."

"My dear friend, don't chew your tongue. Tell me straight, will you take me for your wife or won't you?" And her lovely brow puckered in a sad frown.

So Stepan spoke up.

"I cannot, for I have given my word to another."

He fell silent, staring down at his bast shoes, thinking the Maid would be angry. Yet she seemed pleased.

"You are a good man, my brave Stepanushko. I praised you once, but I have double praise for this. You were not blinded by my riches and you would not trade your Natasha for a maid of stone." (She was quite right; Natasha *was* his sweetheart's name.) "Here, take her this small gift."

And she handed him a malachite casket. Inside were jewels of every kind to take a maiden's fancy: earrings and necklaces and rings—more than the wealthiest bride could ever dream of.

"But how am I to escape from the mine?" asked Stepan.

"Don't worry, just leave that to me. You will be a free man and live in plenty with your young wife. There is just one condition—all thoughts of me must leave your head. That will be my third test. Now come and eat."

When she snapped her fingers, in scuttled the lizards and piled the table high with tasty morsels until it groaned under the weight. She treated him to caviar, salted herring and cucumber, to beetroot soup with sour cream, meat dumplings and thick juicy pancakes, round cheese cakes dripping with cream and sugar, cool rye kvass and honey melon—everything to grace the noblest Russian table.

When he had had his fill, she bade him farewell.

"Stepan, mind you forget me."

Tears suddenly welled in her green eyes and rolled down her cheeks, plip-plop into her hand, there turning to hard green grains. A whole handful.

"Here, take them. Such stones as these are priceless. You will be rich."

The tiny stones were ice cold, but her hand was warm, as if it was a mortal hand, and it trembled a little.

Stepan took the gems, bowing low. His heart was heavy. She pointed her finger and a path opened up, lit by daylight. He wandered along it, passing the glittering underground riches, until at last he found himself back in the bottom-most pit. Once inside, the shaft closed, a lizard fixed the chain back on his leg and all was as before. The jewel casket suddenly shrank and Stepan was able to conceal it inside his shirt. Soon after, the master came to gloat, but instead his eyes grew wide. Stepan's malachite was as fine a grade as could be found anywhere.

"Well, that's strange," he muttered, "there wasn't any here before." He clambered down into the pit to take a good look. "Seems like there's a fortune in this working after all." So he had Stepan replaced by his own nephew.

No sooner had Stepan started work in a new pit than out tumbled the malachite once more. But the nephew got only lumps of clay and rock. Now the master began to get suspicious.

"It can only be one thing. Stepan must have sold his soul to the devil," he thought. He had Stepan unchained and ordered all work at the mine to stop. "Who can tell," he thought to himself, "perhaps the fool was talking sense when he said we should leave the mine." He wrote a letter to the lord who owned the mine, and the lord came in person all the way from the great Russian city of Saint Petersburg. He inspected the malachite, heard the story and summoned Stepan.

"Now, look here, young fellow. I'll set you free if you can find me two solid pieces of malachite tall enough to carve pillars for my palace."

"I cannot promise you for sure," Stepan calmly replied. "We must wait and see if my luck holds."

He did find them, of course. How could he fail, when he now knew every cavern in the mountain and had the Maid herself at his elbow? Tall columns were carved from the malachite, exactly as ordered, hauled to the surface and despatched to the lord's palace.

From then on, Stepan was a free man. But all the riches vanished from the mine, and water seeped in; it rose higher and higher until at last the mine was flooded.

Stepan built himself a fine wooden cottage, married his Natasha, had three children—all, you would think, a man could desire. But no, he brooded and pined away.

Sick as he was, he would often drag himself off towards the old mine—hunting rabbits, he would say. He never caught anything though. Then, one day, in late autumn, he went off for the last time. His family waited and waited... Where had he got to? The villagers eventually found him lying dead by a large moss-green rock near the mine; he seemed to be smiling. Those first on the scene told how they had seen a green lizard with a black-striped tail, such a big one as had never been seen in those parts. It was sitting there over Stepan, its head held high, and tears were trickling down its face. As soon as people came running, it darted behind the rock and vanished.

When they brought Stepan home and began to wash him, they found one fist clenched tight; as they looked closely they could just glimpse something green in it, tiny green grains, a whole handful. One white-bearded man claimed he knew what they were; he peered sideways at the grains in Stepan's fist and said:

"Those are copper emeralds; gems don't come rarer than them, they're worth a fortune. That's a real treasure he's left you, Natasha. But where could he have found them?"

Natasha, Stepan's widow, said he had never mentioned the stones to her. Once he had given her a malachite casket, before they were married; it contained many lovely gems, but none like these.

They set about taking the emeralds from Stepan's fist and, as his fingers uncurled, the stones at once crumbled to dust. So nobody discovered where he had found them. Though digging restarted soon after in the old mine, all they found was brown ore streaked with green, quite worthless.

No one knew that the gems in Stepan's hand were really the tears of the Maid of the Copper Mountain. He had never sold them, nor traded them. He had kept their secret from everyone, and he had taken it with him to the grave.

This is a story from The Malachite Basket, *a wonderful collection of tales from the mineworkers in the Urals. A Russian journalist told me about them, while I was doing promotion in Moscow, as she had read about the stone-skinned Goyl in* Reckless. *The stories inspired the malachite skin of Nerron, one of my favourite characters in that series (I have his mother worship the mistress of the copper mountain). Many of these tales are connected and I hope* The Maid of the Copper Mountain *will inspire many readers to explore the others. I promise it's worth it, whether you read them in a translation from the Russian original or in the retellings of James Riordan.*

The Tale
of the
Firebird

Once upon a time, in a faraway kingdom, lived the great ruler Tsar Vasilyi. He had three sons, and the youngest was named Ivan Tsarevitch. The Tsar's greatest pride was his garden, filled with exotic trees, and in the centre of this garden was the prize of his kingdom: a tree with golden apples.

One day, the Tsar's gardener came to report that someone had been stealing the fruits of the golden apple tree! Every night there were fewer apples left. Determined to catch the thief, the Tsar ordered his three sons to watch his precious garden through the night.

The eldest son was in charge on the first night, but he fell asleep and came back to his father the next day with nothing to report. The second son tried to watch the garden on the second night, but he, too, fell asleep and saw nothing.

On the third night, the youngest, Ivan Tsarevitch, was sent to the garden. He watched until midnight without falling asleep. Just as his eyes were about to close, a sudden flash of light illuminated the entire garden.

A Firebird!

As soon as the Firebird landed on the golden tree, Ivan Tsarevitch grabbed for his tail. That would stop him. But it didn't! The Firebird flew away, leaving Ivan Tsarevitch with a single, glowing feather in his hand.

The Tsar was amazed when he saw the miraculous light of the Firebird's feather. "I must have this Firebird!" he said. "Saddle your horses, my dear sons. Whichever of you can catch the Firebird will have half my kingdom as a reward!"

So the three sons rode off, each going his own way. Whether it was a long way or a short way, we don't know.

Ivan Tsarevitch rode to the edge of a primeval forest, where he met a big grey wolf. "You cannot get the Firebird without me, Ivan Tsarevitch," the wolf said. "Leave your horse here and saddle me instead. You spared my children in the Tsar's wolf hunt last year, so now I will be your servant and your guide."

So Ivan Tsarevitch climbed up on the wolf's back. The wolf made a great leap—all the way up to the birds in the sky. They flew over woods and mountains, over wide rivers, so high that it took Ivan Tsarevitch's breath away.

Whether their way was long or short, we don't know. But at last they arrived at a land of wondrous gardens and crystal palaces.

"Go into the garden, Ivan Tsarevitch," said the wolf. "You will see a Firebird in a golden cage hanging from the branch of a tree. Take the Firebird, but do not touch the golden cage, for it will bring you bad luck."

Ivan Tsarevitch entered the garden and saw the Firebird in its golden cage. As he reached in, the gold was so beautiful that he could not keep himself from touching it. The moment he did, thousands of invisible bells began to ring and an army of guards appeared from nowhere. They grabbed Ivan Tsarevitch and took him to their king—King Muhmud.

Muhmud recognized the Tsar's youngest son. "I would kill any other man who tried to do what you have just done. But your father is my friend. For his sake, I will forgive you. You may keep the Firebird. However, in exchange, you must go to the faraway land of King Karam and bring me back a horse with a golden mane."

Ivan Tsarevitch went back to his wolf and told him what King Muhmud had said. "Don't worry, Ivan Tsarevitch," said the grey wolf. "I can help you find this horse. But I tell you, next time, do not disobey me!"

So Ivan Tsarevitch saddled the wolf again, and in three great leaps they had reached the sky and were soaring above the clouds. They flew over high mountains, deep seas and enormous green lands.

Finally they reached the kingdom of Karam, and the wolf gave Ivan Tsarevitch his instructions. "Go into the king's garden, and you will see a horse grazing on the meadow. Take the horse by its golden mane and bring it here, but do not touch its harness, for it will bring you bad luck."

Ivan Tsarevitch did everything as the wolf told him, but when he saw the harness, its golden beauty was so fascinating that he could not resist the temptation to touch it. As soon as he did, there was a sound of thousands of invisible bells and at the same moment, the guards appeared. They brought Ivan Tsarevitch to see King Karam.

King Karam looked at Ivan Tsarevitch with menacing eyes. "Who are you? Why do you want my horse?" Ivan Tsarevitch told the king his story, holding back no secrets.

Karam said, "I will give you this horse and his golden harness as a gift—but in return you must go to the kingdom beyond all other kingdoms, the kingdom of Koshchei the Immortal, and bring my sister, Yelena the Beautiful, back to me. Since her capture three years ago, my suffering has been endless. Many heroes have lost their heads on Koshchei's field on her account. May God help you! Go!"

Ivan Tsarevitch came back to his wolf in low spirits and told him what had passed. "Don't despair, Ivan

Tsarevitch—a man can die but once," said the wolf. "Get ready to go on another journey. I know who can help us."

So Ivan Tsarevitch saddled the grey wolf once again, and they rushed as fast as they could to the kingdom beyond all other kingdoms, the kingdom of Koshchei the Immortal. They flew over dark woods and impassable swamps.

"Now we are coming to the place where no human has ever set foot," said the grey wolf. "Baba Yaga the Wicked dwells here. If you want to find Yelena the Beautiful, you must do everything Baba Yaga tells you."

Ivan Tsarevitch turned and saw a cottage that spun around on chicken feet in the middle of the dark forest. It spun so fast that he could not see the door to enter. After consulting with the wolf, Ivan Tsarevitch stood before the cottage and shouted, "Little hut, little hut, show your front to me and your back to the woods!"

The cottage immediately stopped spinning and settled down on its chicken feet with its door facing Ivan Tsarevitch. He was about to knock at the door when he heard a great thunderclap and Baba Yaga the Wicked suddenly appeared.

"Why have you come to visit me, Ivan Tsarevitch?" she cackled. "I think I know. I will help you—if you are brave!" Baba Yaga gave a shout, and from all corners of the forest, creatures came running: satyrs, monsters and other beasts. Baba Yaga ordered them to build a fire and put on a huge cauldron of magical waters and herbs. When this witch's brew began to boil, she ordered Ivan Tsarevitch to take off his clothes and bathe himself in the bubbling cauldron.

Ivan Tsarevitch crossed himself... and jumped in.

And then—a miracle! Instead of being boiled like a shrimp, Ivan Tsarevitch found himself in the cool water of a forest lake. In the middle of the lake was a little island covered with sedge and moss, and deep in the moss was a glimmer of something shining.

He pushed the sedge away. There was a dazzling sword. As soon as Ivan Tsarevitch touched its hilt, a magical strength came to him.

Ivan Tsarevitch stood up and found himself at the edge of the forest, still holding the magical sword. His faithful wolf was waiting for him, all ready with his clothes.

"You did a good job this time, Ivan Tsarevitch," he said.

Faster than the wind they reached the sky, and in the blink of an eye they were approaching the castle of Koshchei. The moment they touched the ground, they heard the sound of a horn and saw Koshchei the Immortal riding up on his horse.

"I am looking for the sister of King Karam," Ivan Tsarevitch said, with his sword resting before him.

But Koshchei gave a sinister laugh. "I can't fight a man without a horse! Are you not the son of the Tsar? Yet so poor that you don't have a horse?"

Ivan Tsarevitch didn't know what to answer, but the grey wolf whispered, "Don't worry. I will help you." In a moment, the wolf had transformed himself into a warrior's horse so great and strong that it cannot be described, either with words or with a brush.

Koshchei the Immortal stopped laughing. Ivan Tsarevitch mounted the great warrior horse and drew his magical sword. The battle began.

Ten times they drew their swords and charged at each other. But their strengths were evenly matched, and neither could win.

Then, just as Ivan Tsarevitch was about to make another charge, he spotted Yelena the Beautiful. Her beauty gave him a jolt of power, and his strength was suddenly doubled. Ivan Tsarevitch attacked Koshchei once more with his magical sword and struck him with a final, deadly blow.

That was the end of the evil Koshchei, for evil cannot be immortal. Only love can be immortal.

Yelena the Beautiful and Ivan Tsarevitch fell in love at first sight. Yelena the Beautiful made a wreath of field flowers and crowned Ivan Tsarevitch. Then they saddled the mighty warrior horse, and in less than a moment, they had arrived at the kingdom of Karam.

Karam ran out of his palace to meet them. Tears streamed from his eyes at the sight of his beloved sister. He embraced her and Ivan Tsarevitch together, saying, "I bless your love, my dear children. I am giving my kingdom to you, Ivan Tsarevitch, and I want you to be its ruler when I am old."

Ivan Tsarevitch thanked Karam for his generous gifts and went off to fulfil the rest of his promises. He saddled the horse with the golden mane for Yelena and mounted his warrior horse beside her.

Together they rode to the kingdom of Muhmud. King Muhmud and all of his glorious court were overjoyed to see Ivan Tsarevitch again and amazed with the beauty of Yelena. The king was so taken with her that he gave her the golden-maned horse. He congratulated Ivan Tsarevitch on his great happiness and gave him the gift he had promised—the Firebird in its golden cage.

When Ivan Tsarevitch and Yelena the Beautiful returned to the king's stables, they found that the warrior horse had transformed itself back into a grey wolf once again. "Here my help ends, Ivan Tsarevitch. Be happy!" Ivan Tsarevitch thanked him, and the wolf vanished into the dark woods.

Tsar Vasilyi was very happy to see his beloved son with Yelena the Beautiful and all the kingly gifts they had been given. The wedding was declared and the Tsar gave a feast for everyone in the kingdom, brightened by the light of the Firebird. For many, many years afterwards, the people in that part of the world still talked of the wedding feast of the Tsar's youngest son and of the magical power and beauty of the Firebird.

When I started my fairy-tale journey around the world for Reckless, *I began in familiar territory. The first book,* The Petrified Flesh, *plays with motifs from* The Grimm's Tales *I grew up with. The second book,* Living Shadows, *quotes tales from France, England and Switzerland, most of them less known but some as iconic as* Bluebeard *or* Puss in Boots, *although a French journalist told me: "Cornelia, we have forgotten our fairy tales." Nevertheless I still felt I was in familiar territory.*

I definitely left familiarity behind when I travelled East in Book Three and read fairy tales from Ukraine, Russia, Siberia, Mongolia or Kazakhstan. Naturally, in these I met many themes one finds in fairy tales all over the world, but the taste of these tales was distinctly different. Not only did many stories feature powerful female heroines but the landscapes that inspired them were vast and so different from the ones we travel in German or French fairy tales. And certainly no Russian journalist would ever say these tales were forgotten. On the contrary, one journalist told me that her grandson got better when she read Pushkin's fairy tales to him in hospital. Pushkin's tales... I think part of the reason why Russia still embraces its old folk tales so passionately is the fact that Alexander Pushkin retold them so brilliantly—adding a few elements from Arabian tales, as he was very proud of his Moorish blood. Pushkin, not Tolstoy or Dostoevsky, is the Russians' favourite writer, and surely not only because he died such a romantic death in a duel.

Bluebeard

Once upon a time there lived a man who possessed fine houses in town and in the country, dishes and plates of silver and gold, furniture all covered in embroidery, and carriages all gilded; but unfortunately the man's beard was blue, and this made him so ugly and fearsome that all the women and girls, without exception, would run away from him. Nearby there lived a noble lady, who had two daughters of the greatest beauty. The man asked her permission to marry one or other of them, leaving it to her to decide which daughter she would give to him. Neither of them wanted him, and each said that the other one could be his wife, for they could not bring themselves to marry a man with a blue beard. What put them off even more was that he had already been married several times, and nobody knew what had become of the wives.

Bluebeard, in order to get better acquainted, took them and their mother, with three or four of their best friends and some young men who lived in the neighbourhood, to visit one of his country houses, where they stayed for a whole week. They had outings all the time, hunting parties, fishing trips and banquets; nor did they ever go to sleep, but spent all the night playing practical jokes on one another; and they enjoyed themselves so much that the younger of the two sisters began to think that their host's beard was not as blue as it had been, and that he was just what a gentleman should be. As soon as they were back in town, it was settled that they should marry.

After a month had passed, Bluebeard told his wife that he had to go away for at least six weeks to another part of the country, on an important business matter. He told her to make sure that she enjoyed herself properly while he was away, to invite her friends to stay and to take them out into the country if she wanted to, and not to stint herself wherever she was. "Here are the keys of the two big storerooms," he said, "the keys for the cupboards with the gold and silver dinner service that is not for every day, and for my strongboxes with my gold and silver coins, and for my jewel boxes, and here is the master key for all the rooms. As for this small key here, it will unlock the private room at the end of the long gallery in my apartment downstairs. You may open everything and go everywhere, except for this private room, where I forbid you to go; and I forbid it to you so absolutely that, if you did happen to go into it, there is no knowing what I might do, so angry would I be." She promised to obey his commands exactly; and he kissed her, got into his carriage and set off on his journey.

Her neighbours and friends came to visit the new bride without waiting to be invited, so impatient were they to see all the expensive things in the house; they had not dared to come while her husband was there, because of his blue beard, which scared them. And off they went to look at the bedrooms, the sitting rooms and the dressing rooms, each one finer and more luxurious than the one before. Then they went up to the storerooms, and words failed them when they saw how many beautiful things there were: tapestries, beds, sofas, armchairs, side tables, dining tables, and mirrors so tall that you could see yourself from head to foot, some with frames of glass, some of silver and some of silver gilt, which were the most beautiful and splendid that they had ever seen. They kept on saying how lucky their friend was and how much they envied her; she, however, took no pleasure in the sight of all this wealth, because of the impatience that she felt to go and open the door to the private room downstairs.

So keen was her curiosity that, without reflecting how rude it was to leave her guests, she went down by a little secret staircase at the back; and she was in such a hurry that two or three times she nearly broke her neck. When the door of the little room was in front of her she stood looking at it for a while, remembering how her husband had forbidden her to open it, and wondering whether something bad might happen to her if she disobeyed, but the temptation was strong and she could not resist it; so she took the little key and, trembling all over, opened the door. At first she could see nothing, because the shutters were closed. After a few moments, she began to see that the floor was all covered in clotted blood, and that it reflected the bodies of several women, dead, and tied up along the wall (they were the wives whom Bluebeard had married, and whose throats he had cut one after the other). She nearly died of fright, and the key, which she had taken out of the lock, fell out of her hand.

When she had recovered herself a little, she picked up the key again, and locking the door behind her she went upstairs to her room to try to collect her thoughts, but she was unable to, because the shock had been too great. She noticed that the key was stained with blood, and although she cleaned it two or three times the blood would not go away. However much she washed it, and even scoured it with sand and pumice, the blood stayed on it; it was a magic key, and there was no way of cleaning it completely: when the blood was removed from one side, it came back on the other.

Bluebeard returned from his journey that very night, saying that while he was still on his way, he had received letters telling him that the business he had gone to arrange had already been settled to his advantage. His wife did all she could to make him believe that she was delighted at his returning so soon. The next day, he asked for his keys back, and she gave them to him, but her hand was trembling so much that he easily guessed what had happened.

"Why is it," he asked, "that the key to my private room is not here with the others?"

She replied: "I must have left it upstairs on my table."

"Then don't forget to give it to me later," said Bluebeard.

She made excuses several times, but finally she had to bring him the key. Bluebeard examined it, and said to his wife: "Why is there blood on this key?"

"I know nothing about it," said the poor woman, as pale as death.

"You know nothing about it?" said Bluebeard; "but I do—you have tried to get into my private room. Very well, madam, that is where you will go; and there you will take your place, beside the ladies you have seen."

She threw herself at her husband's feet, weeping and pleading to be forgiven, and all her actions showed how truly she repented being so disobedient. So beautiful was she, and in such distress, that she would have moved the very rocks to pity; but Bluebeard's heart was harder than rock. "You must die, madam," he said, "this very instant."

"If I must die," she said, looking at him with her eyes full of tears, "give me some time to say my prayers to God."

"I will give you ten minutes," said Bluebeard, "and not a moment longer."

As soon as she was alone, she called to her sister and said: "Sister Anne" (for that was her name), "go up to the top of the tower, I beg you, to see if my brothers are coming, for they promised to come today; and if you can see them, make them a signal to hurry."

Her sister Anne went to the top of the tower, and the poor woman below cried up to her at every moment: "*What can you see, sister Anne, sister Anne? Is anyone coming this way?*"

And her sister would reply: "*All I can see is the dust in the sun, and the green of the grass all round.*"

Meanwhile, Bluebeard, holding a great cutlass in his hand, shouted as loud as he could to his wife: "Come down from there at once, or else I'll come and fetch you."

"Please, just a minute longer," his wife answered, and immediately called out, but quietly: "*What can you see, sister Anne, sister Anne? Is anyone coming this way?*"

And her sister Anne replied: "*All I can see is the dust in the sun, and the green of the grass all round.*"

"Down you come at once," Bluebeard was shouting, "or I will fetch you down."

"I'm coming now," his wife kept saying; and then she would call: "*What can you see, sister Anne, sister Anne? Is anyone coming this way?*"

And then her sister Anne replied: "I can see a great cloud of dust, and it is coming towards us."

"Is that our brothers on their way?"

"Alas! sister, no; it is only a flock of sheep."

"Do you refuse to come down?" shouted Bluebeard.

"Just a moment more," his wife answered, and called out: "*What can you see, sister Anne, sister Anne? Is anyone coming this way?*"

"I can see," she replied, "two horsemen riding towards us, but they are still a long way off... God be praised," she cried a moment later, "it's our brothers; I shall wave to them as hard as I can, so that they will hurry."

Bluebeard began to shout so loudly that the whole house shook. His poor wife came down, and fell at his feet in tears, with her hair all dishevelled. "That will not save you," cried Bluebeard; "you must die." And taking her hair in one hand and raising his cutlass in the air with the other, he was on the point of chopping off her head. The poor woman, turning towards him and looking at him with despair in her eyes, begged him to give her a minute or two to prepare herself for death.

"No, no," he said, "commend your soul to God," and raising his arm...

At that moment, there was heard such a loud banging at the door that Bluebeard stopped short; the door opened, and at once the two horsemen came in; they drew their swords and ran straight at Bluebeard. He recognized them for his wife's brothers: one was a dragoon guard, the other a musketeer; immediately he ran to escape, but the two brothers went after him so fast that they caught him before he could get out of the front door. They cut him open with their swords, and left him dead. His poor wife was almost as dead as her husband, without even enough strength to get up and embrace her two brothers.

It turned out that Bluebeard had no heirs, so that his wife became the mistress of all his riches. She used some to marry her sister Anne to a young gentleman who had loved her for years; some she used to buy captains' commissions for her two brothers; and the remainder, to marry herself to a man of true worth, with whom she forgot all about the bad time she had had with Bluebeard.

People with sense who use their eyes,
Study the world and know its ways,
Will not take long to realize
That this is a tale of bygone days,
And what it tells is now untrue:
Whether his beard be black or blue,
The modern husband does not ask
His wife to undertake a task
Impossible for her to do,
And even when dissatisfied,
With her he's quiet as a mouse.
It isn't easy to decide
Which is the master in the house.

This is one of the tales I used as direct inspiration for a character in Reckless. *I made the Bluebeards into their own species and used the motif of desire far more than the original tale does. My Bluebeard seduces with beauty and charm whereas in the French tale he is ugly and needs to convince the mother of his future bride with money and influence to give him her daughter.*

The central motif of the original tale is in fact obedience and the unveiling of secrets. I was never quite sure what this tale was supposed to teach women. That they should accept their husband's secrets—even if that secret is a room with the bloody corpses of their predecessors—so they don't endanger marital bliss? That death is a just punishment for a wife who doesn't obey her husband's instructions? Or is it a warning to not pick a man just for his riches?

As always in fairy tales, all of these may be true. And underneath all its sexist and conservative layers, the tale of the Bluebeard is also and once again a source of powerful imagery. The One Door that cannot be opened. The Magic Key that stays bloodstained and thereby reveals the crime it's supposed to keep hidden. And then, of course, the Blue Beard, a sign that the dark hero of the tale has a somewhat otherworldly origin. Yes, maybe Bluebeard is not a human man after all (as I claim in Reckless), but someone so wild and dangerous that the tale also warns women to not fall for exotic foreigners.

Oh, yes, I should of course also mention Gilles de Rais and Conomor the Accursed, murderers who may have been the historical inspiration for this tale. Which brings us to the fascinating question of whether all fairy tales were inspired by true events, with time adding layers of meaning and magic...

The
Six Swans

Once upon a time, a king was hunting in a great wood, and he pursued a wild animal so eagerly that none of his people could follow him. When evening came, he stood still, and looking around him, he found that he had lost his way, and seeking a path, he found none. Then all at once he saw an old woman with a wagging head coming up to him, and it was a witch.

"Good woman," he said to her, "can you show me the way through this wood?"

"Oh yes, king," she answered, "certainly I can, but I must make a condition, and if you do not fulfil it, you will never get out of the wood again, and will die of hunger here."

"What is the condition?" asked the king.

"I have a daughter," said the old woman, "who is as fair as any in the world, and if you will take her for your bride, and make her queen, I will show you the way out of the wood."

The king consented, because of the difficulty he was in, and the old woman led him into her little house, where her daughter was sitting by the fire.

She received the king as if she had been expecting him, and though he saw that she was very beautiful, she did not please him, and he could not look at her without an inward shudder. After he had lifted the maiden up on to his horse, the old woman showed him the way, and he reached his royal castle, where the wedding was held.

The king had been married before, and had seven children from his first wife, six boys and one girl, whom he loved more than anything in the world. As he was afraid the stepmother might not treat them well, and perhaps would do them harm, he took them to a lonely castle in the middle of a wood. It was so well hidden, and the road to it was so hard to find, that the king himself could not have found it had it not been for a ball of yarn with wondrous properties that a wise woman had given him. Whenever he threw it down before him, it unrolled itself and showed him the way.

And the king went so often to see his dear children that the queen noticed his absences. She became curious and wanted to know what he did alone out in the wood so often. She bribed his servants with much money, and they told her the secret, and told her of the ball of yarn which alone could show the way. And she did not find rest until she had discovered where the king kept the yarn, and then she made little shirts of white silk, and as she had learnt witchcraft from her mother, she sewed a spell into them.

And once, when the king had ridden to the hunt, she took the little shirts and went into the wood, and the ball of yarn showed her the way.

The children, seeing someone in the distance, thought it was their beloved father coming to see them, and they came to meet him, jumping with joy. Then the wicked queen threw over each one of the little shirts, and as the shirts touched their bodies, they were transformed into swans, and flew away over the wood.

So the queen went home very pleased to think she had got rid of her stepchildren, but the girl had not run out with her brothers, and so the queen knew nothing about her.

The next day, the king went to see his children, but he found only his daughter.

"Where are your brothers?" asked the king.

"Ah, dear father," answered she. "They have gone away and have left me behind." And she told him how from her window she had seen her brothers fly away through the wood as swans. And she showed him the feathers which they had dropped in the courtyard, and which she had picked up.

The king grieved, but he never thought that it was the queen who had done this evil deed, and since he feared the girl might also be stolen from him, he wanted to take her away with him. But she was afraid of the stepmother, and begged the king to let her remain one more night in the castle in the wood.

Then she said to herself, *I must stay here no longer, but go and seek my brothers.*

And when the night came, she fled straight into the wood. She went on all night and the next day, until she could go on no longer. At last she saw a rude hut, and she entered and found a room with six little beds in it; she did not dare to lie down in one, but she crept under one and lay on the hard boards and wished for night.

When the sun was almost setting, she heard a rustling sound, and saw six swans come flying in through the window. They sat on the ground, and blew at one another until they had blown all their feathers off, and their swan skin stripped off like a shirt. And the girl looked at them and recognized her brothers, and she was very glad, and crept out from under the bed. The brothers were no less glad when they saw their sister, but their joy did not last long.

"You must not stay here," they said to her. "This is a robbers' den, and when they come and find you here, they will kill you."

"But can't you defend me?" asked the little sister.

"No," they answered, "for we can only get rid of our swan skins and keep our human shape every evening for a quarter of an hour, and after that we must be changed again into swans."

Their sister wept at hearing this, and said, "Can nothing be done to set you free?"

"Oh no," answered they, "the conditions would be too hard. You would not be allowed to speak or laugh for six whole years, and in that time you'd have to sew six little shirts out of blue star flowers. If one single word came out of your mouth, all your work would be lost."

And just as the brothers had told her this, the quarter of an hour was over, and they changed into swans and flew out of the window.

But the girl made up her mind to set her brothers free, even if it were to cost her life. She left the hut, and, going into the middle of the wood, she climbed a tree and spent the night there.

The next morning, she set to work and gathered star flowers and began sewing. There was no one to speak to, and she was in no mood for laughing, so she sat there and looked at nothing but her work.

When she had been going on like this for a long time, the king of that country happened to go hunting in that wood, and some of his huntsmen came up to the tree in which the girl was sitting.

They called out to her, saying, "Who are you?"

But she gave no answer.

"Come down," they cried. "We do not want to harm you."

She just shook her head. And when they pressed her further with questions, she threw down her gold necklace, hoping they would be content with that.

But they would not leave off, so she threw her girdle down to them, and when that was no good, her garters, then one thing after another from everything she had on and could possibly spare, until she had nothing left but her smock.

But still the huntsmen would not be put off, and they climbed the tree, brought the girl down and led her to the king.

The king asked, "Who are you? What are you doing up in that tree?"

But she did not answer.

He asked her in all the languages he knew, but she remained mute as a fish. But because she was so beautiful, the king's heart was touched and he felt a great love grow for her. He put his coat around her, and sat her before him on his horse and brought her to his castle.

Then he had her dressed in rich clothing, and her beauty radiated as bright as daylight, but she could not be brought to utter a word.

He seated her by his side at his table, and her modesty and gentle expression pleased him so much that he said, "I desire to marry you, and no other in the whole world." And after a few days he married her.

But the king had a wicked mother, who was displeased with the marriage and spoke ill of the young queen.

"Who knows where that strumpet came from?" she said. "And she cannot speak a word! She is not worthy of a king!"

After a year had passed, and the queen had brought her first child into the world, the old woman carried it away, and dabbed the queen's mouth with blood as she slept. Then she went to the king and declared that his wife was a cannibal. The king did not want to believe such a thing, and ordered that no one should harm her. And the queen went on quietly sewing the shirts, paying attention to nothing else.

The next time she gave birth, to a fine boy, the wicked mother-in-law worked the same deceit, but the king could not make himself believe her words.

He said, "She is too pious and good to do such a thing, and if she were not mute, and could defend herself, her innocence would be as clear as day."

When the old woman stole away a newborn child for the third time and accused the queen, who was unable to say a word in her defence, the king could do nothing else but give her up to the court, and it sentenced her to death by fire.

The day on which her sentence was to be carried out was also the last day of the six years during which she could neither speak nor laugh, and she had freed her dear brothers from the power of the evil spell. The six shirts were complete; only one was missing its left sleeve. And when the queen was led to the pyre, she carried the six shirts in her arms. She stood atop the pyre and, as the fire was about to be kindled, she looked around and there were six swans flying through the air. She saw that their deliverance was near, and her heart raced with joy.

The swans flew up to her with rushing wings, and lowered themselves, so she could throw the shirts over them; and as they were touched by them, the swan skins fell off, and her brothers stood before her in the flesh, and they were fresh and beautiful. The youngest was missing the left arm and instead had one swan wing on his back.

They embraced and kissed each other, and the queen went up to the king, who was stunned by all this, and she began to speak to him and said, "Dearest husband, now I may speak and reveal to you that I am innocent, and have been falsely accused."

And she told him of the treachery of the stepmother, who had taken away and hidden her three children. But then they were brought forth, causing the king to feel great joy, and the mother-in-law was bound to the pyre and burnt to ashes.

And the king and queen, with her six brothers, lived for many years in peace and joy.

When asked about my favourite fairy tales, I always name this story, though I can't explain why it is such a favourite. I guess it's just further proof that the enchantment fairy tales cast reaches deep into our subconscious—or maybe even deeper, into memories older than ourselves, stored away in our bones.

There are, once again, plenty of reasons to not like the story. Look at the women! There is, inevitably, the scheming witch and her equally evil daughter. The daughters of witches are always evil, as if that quality is passed on with the blood (witches rarely have sons). I made them a different species in Reckless, not evil by nature, but practising white or dark magic by choice.

The witches who burnt at the stakes of our world were very human women, of course. There is a theory that their knowledge about birth control was the reason for burning them. It was not only the worldly rulers but the church who had a desperate need for more soldiers—a need that doesn't coincide with birth control. Once the witches were gone, women regularly gave birth to ten or even more children as there was no knowledge left about how to prevent or interrupt pregnancies. The knowledge about healing plants, the medicine of the poor, had been burnt as well, and the only available healers were male doctors who were not affordable for the poor.

The so-called witches were often women who lived alone, without men, in the woods, connected to nature in a way that men found almost as frightening as the freedom those women claimed. So, yes, of course they were evil.

The heroine in The Six Swans *is not a witch. At first sight she seems quite unappealing in her silence and inability to defend herself. So why, Cornelia, did you always love this story?*

There is a strength in that girl that fascinated me. I could see her so vividly, sewing the shirts for her cursed brothers. In the version I remember she made them from nettles that burnt her fingers. I fell into burning nettles quite a few times as a child and her ability to ignore that pain vastly impressed me. As did her will to not speak and keep her vow even when she was sent to the stake. And then the image of the brothers, flying over the stake, their sister throwing the shirts up to them, although one is still missing a sleeve.

The magic of fairy tales is not in their words. It's in the images their words summon. We do underestimate the power of visual thinking nowadays, although we are being seduced by images every day, be it in commercials or on political posters. Abstract thought finds it very hard to express all the layers one image can hold. Those shirts, or Cinderella's shoe, the spindle of Sleeping Beauty, not to mention all the monsters we meet in fairy tales... Images can hold so many layers of meaning, many of them invisible. They can express contradictory truths so much easier than words, vague fears and hopes, wordless pain...

Terry Gilliam demonstrates this masterfully in his movie The Fisher King, *when Robin Williams's character flees from the Red Knight through the streets of New York in a brilliant visual incarnation of the terrible grief he feels about the murder of his wife. Fairy tales work like that. They throw images in our path, like the one of the brother whose arm remains a swan wing. Of course it is the youngest brother, and so much can be read into this one image.*

This brother was the inspiration for the Man-Swans in Reckless. *As a child I probably thought he was the lucky one because at least he could keep one wing. I still do.*

Golden
Foot

Once there lived a blacksmith in the hamlet of Pont-de-Pîle on the shores of the Lac de Gers. He was at least a fathom tall and as strong as a pair of oxen. The man was blacker than his hearth, with a long beard, ragged hair and smouldering red eyes. Never did he set foot in a church, and he ate meat every day, even on Good Friday. It was said that the blacksmith of Pont-de-Pîle was not Christian.

The truth was that he lived alone in a house which none was permitted to enter. Whoever required the master had to call him out. The blacksmith was without equal in working metals, be they gold or silver. Orders fell his way like hailstones. He completed all work without help, bar that of a black wolf. The creature was as big as a horse and lived locked up day and night in the wheel that moved the bellows at the forge. Seven young lads had come to the master to learn his trade. But the trials were so hard, so hard, that they all died by the third day.

At that same time, a poor widow lived alone with her son in the hamlet of La Côte, between Lectoure and Pont-de-Pîle.

When the lad was fourteen years of age, he said to his mother, "Mother, we are both working ourselves to death, yet we never come by more than the very least we need to live on. Tomorrow I shall seek out the blacksmith of Pont-de-Pîle and ask to be his apprentice."

"My son, that man never sets foot in a church. He eats meat every day, even on Good Friday. It is said that he is not Christian."

"Mother, the blacksmith of Pont-de-Pîle shall not tempt me to evil."

"My son, seven young lads have sought him out to learn his trade. But the trials were so hard, so hard, that they died by the third day."

"Mother, I shall pass his trials and shall not die of them."

"My son, I trust in God's grace and in the Holy Virgin Mary."

Both went to sleep.

The next morning at dawn, the lad stood in front of the forge of Pont-de-Pîle.

"Ho! Blacksmith of Pont-de-Pîle! Ho! Ho! Ho!"

"What do you want, lad?"

"I want to become your apprentice, blacksmith of Pont-de-Pile."

"Then enter, lad!"

The lad stepped inside the workshop, and he felt neither fear nor dread.

"Show me that you're strong, lad!"

The lad took an anvil weighing seven hundredweights, and he threw it over a hundred fathoms wide.

"Show me that you're deft, lad!"

The lad went to a large cobweb and untangled it from beginning to end, winding it into a single clew without ever tearing the thread.

"Show me that you're brave, lad!"

The lad opened the hatch to the wheel wherein the wolf that was as big as a horse lived day and night to drive the bellows of the forge. The wolf jumped out at once, but the lad plucked the beast from the air by its neck, hewed off its tail and four claws on the anvil and burnt it alive in the forge.

"Lad, you have passed the trial. You are strong, and deft, and brave. You shall begin in three days. I pay a good wage. But you may neither live nor eat here."

"Master, I will obey you."

The apprentice bid goodbye to the blacksmith of Pont-de-Pile and walked out. Then he thought, *My mother is right. My master is a man unlike any other. Three days and nights I shall conceal myself and watch him in secret. Then I shall know who I am dealing with.*

Having decided this, the apprentice went to see his mother.

"Mother, we are rich. The blacksmith of Pont-de-Pîle has employed me as his apprentice. I shall take up my duties in three days' time. I shall not command you, Mother, but give me a satchel of bread and a bottle of wine. I have to make a journey, and I need to depart in haste so I may return in time."

"Here, my son. May the Good Lord and the Holy Virgin keep you from evil."

The apprentice bid his mother farewell and made as though he were embarking on a journey.

But he concealed himself in a hayloft near the forge of Pont-de-Pîle, and from there he saw and heard everything without being seen or heard himself.

At sunset, the blacksmith of Pont-de-Pîle locked up his shop. But his apprentice did not trust him, so he kept his eyes and ears open.

As the stars showed the eleventh hour, the blacksmith of Pont-de-Pîle quietly opened the door of his house and checked that no one was watching. Then he mimicked the call of a cricket.

"*Cree, cree, cree.* Come, fair daughter. Come, Snake Queen. *Cree, cree, cree.*"

"Father, I am here."

The Snake Queen was tall and as thick as a sack of wheat. On her head she wore a black lily blossom. Father and daughter greeted and caressed each other with great joy.

"Well, Father, do you have an apprentice?"

"In three days I shall have one, fair daughter. He is the son of the widow of La Côte. He is strong, and he is deft, and he is brave."

"I have seen him, Father. I love him."

"Good, fair daughter. When he is old enough, you shall marry him. Now go. Midnight is near, and I scarcely have time to make ready."

The Snake Queen left. And soon the blacksmith of Pont-de-Pîle went to the shores of the Lac de Gers, to a meadow surrounded by poplar, willow and ash.

The apprentice had slipped out of the hayloft. He followed his master quietly, very quietly, concealing himself behind the trees.

The blacksmith of Pont-de-Pîle undressed until he was as naked as a worm, and hid his garments in the hollow of a willow. Then he slipped off his skin from head to toe until he stood as a tall otter.

"I shall hide my human skin well," he said, "for should I not find it before sunrise, I should have to remain an otter for eternity."

He hid his man skin in the hollow of the willow, and just as the stars showed the midnight hour, he jumped into the Lac de Gers. The apprentice saw him swim and dive to the bottom of the lake and return with a carp and an eel, which he devoured in the moonlight. This went on until dawn. Then the blacksmith of Pont-de-Pîle slipped on his human skin and his garments and returned to his home, never suspecting that he was being observed.

The apprentice again concealed himself in the hayloft. For two more nights he saw and heard what he had seen and heard on that first night.

"So my master is the father of the Snake Queen," he said. "Every night she goes to him and speaks with him. The Snake Queen loves me, and she wants to marry me when I am old enough. My master is doomed to turn into an otter from midnight to dawn. This is all useful to know, but I shall not tell it to anyone."

On the morning of the third day, the apprentice stepped into the workshop. His face was innocent, as though he had seen nothing and heard nothing.

"Good morning, master," he said. "Here I am, ready to begin my apprenticeship."

And so he learnt. At the age of fifteen the apprentice already knew more than his master. But he pretended to be clumsy so as not to arouse the jealousy of the blacksmith of Pont-de-Pîle.

One evening, the master spoke to his apprentice. "Listen! In three months, the Marquis of Fimarcon will wed his daughter to the King of the Sea Isles. The bride needs a lot of jewellery, which I shall create. You will travel ahead with the tools. There will be enough silver and gold, as well as diamonds and gemstones, in the castle of Lagarde. Forge and fit the pieces as well as you can. Do the rough work. One month before the wedding I shall come to see that everything is in order and to complete the many things you could never do on your own."

"Master, I shall obey."

The following morning, the apprentice arrived with his tools at the castle of Lagarde. Straight after breakfast he set to work. There was more than enough gold and silver, as well as diamonds and gemstones.

Oh, master, he thought, *the time has come where you shall see whether there really are many things I could never do on my own.*

And the apprentice worked the gold and silver. He fitted the diamonds and gemstones. Never had there been so many beautiful rings, such beautiful chains, such beautiful earrings, and never shall their like be seen again.

All the masters and servants at the castle of Lagarde praised the apprentice, with the exception of the marquis's youngest daughter. She was a small maiden, as pretty as the day and as modest as a saint. Yet every day, from dawn to dusk, she watched the apprentice work. Then, one day, when they were alone, the maiden spoke.

"Apprentice, beautiful apprentice, you make such beautiful things for my eldest sister. Would your work be even more beautiful if it were for another girl? Pray tell."

"Yes, fair maiden. If I had a loved one, I would make her a gold chain unlike any other."

"Apprentice, beautiful apprentice, what would that gold chain look like? Pray tell."

"Fair maiden, for my loved one I would make a gold chain, a beautiful chain of yellow gold as bright as the sun. I would take that chain from the hot flue, glowing, and I would cool it in a bowl of my own blood. And so hardened, I would throw it into the flue again while my loved one undressed herself to her girdle. Then I would place the beautiful gold chain around her neck, and it would become one with her flesh so that neither god nor devil may ever tear it from her. Thus the beautiful gold chain would make her mine, and she would think of me alone. As long as I am well, the beautiful chain would be bright and golden. But should I be met with misfortune, the chain would turn as red as blood. Then my loved one would have three days to make herself ready. She would say to her parents, 'I must die. Bury me in my wedding dress, with the veil and a wreath of orange blossoms on my head, and some white roses on my belt.' On the third day she would sleep. Everyone would believe her dead. They would bury her, and she would sleep as long as the misfortune hung over me. If I died, she would be lost. But if the misfortune passed, I would wake her and we would be wed."

"Apprentice, beautiful apprentice, forge me this beautiful gold chain!"

After seven hours, the beautiful chain of yellow gold was complete. It shone like the sun. Then the apprentice cast it into the red-hot flue. He took his knife and cut his arm and let the blood flow into a bowl. He put the gold chain in the blood until it was hardened. Then he cast it back into the flue and pumped the bellows while the little maiden undressed to her girdle. Then he placed the beautiful gold chain around her neck and it became one with her flesh so that neither god nor devil could have torn it off her.

"Apprentice, beautiful apprentice, I am your loved one. Now, thanks to this beautiful gold chain, I belong to you and shall think of you alone."

The little maiden returned to her chamber. Neither her parents nor her servants ever learnt what had happened.

The following morning, the blacksmith of Pont-de-Pîle arrived.

"Good morning, master."

"Good morning, apprentice. You have worked for two months now. I have come to see what you have done and to complete the many things you could never do yourself."

"Look, master."

And the apprentice showed the wrought gold and silver, the fitted diamonds and gemstones, the beautiful rings, beautiful chains and earrings.

The blacksmith of Pont-de-Pîle laughed out loud. "Apprentice, there is nothing left for me to teach you. You know more than me. You are now free to open your own forge. But you would do me a service if you stayed three more months."

"Master, I obey. I will stay with you as long as you want."

Then the blacksmith of Pont-de-Pîle and the apprentice went to see the Marquis of Fimarcon.

"Good day, Marquis of Fimarcon."

"Good day, friends. What do you want from me?"

"Marquis of Fimarcon," said the blacksmith of Pont-de-Pîle, "we have nothing left to do here. My apprentice worked better than I ever could have—you must pay *him*."

"Here, apprentice, are a thousand louis d'ors."

"Marquis of Fimarcon, I want no payment. If the thousand louis d'ors are a bother to you then give them to the poor."

They both bid farewell to the Marquis of Fimarcon and returned to Pont-de-Pîle.

Seven days later, the master spoke to his apprentice, "Apprentice, today is the fair at Condom. We have to be there on time. Let's drink a glass and get moving."

"To your health, master."

"To yours, apprentice."

But the blacksmith of Pont-de-Pîle only pretended to drink, for he had put a sleeping potion in the wine which was so strong, so strong, that the apprentice dropped to the ground like a log. Then the blacksmith of Pont-de-Pîle tied up his hands and feet with ropes and chains. He gagged him with a rag.

When the apprentice woke, he saw the forge burning like hell itself and the blacksmith of Pont-de-Pîle was sharpening the teeth of a new saw.

"Apprentice, oh, wretched apprentice, you wanted to know more than your master. Now you are in my power and nobody will free you. You shall suffer and die if you don't obey me. Do you want to marry my daughter, the Snake Queen?"

The mouth of the apprentice was sealed with the gag, so he shook his head to say "no".

Then the blacksmith of Pont-de-Pîle took his new saw. Slowly, very slowly, he sawed off the apprentice's left foot and burnt it in the forge.

"Apprentice, do you want to marry my daughter, the Snake Queen?"

The apprentice shook his head to say "no".

The blacksmith of Pont-de-Pîle picked up his saw again. Slowly, very slowly, he sawed off the apprentice's right foot and burnt it in the forge.

"Apprentice, do you want to marry my daughter, the Snake Queen?"

The apprentice shook his head to say "no".

The blacksmith of Pont-de-Pîle realized that he had wasted his time. He threw the apprentice on his cart and covered him with straw, then he whipped his horse, and it ran off like lightning.

When the sun set, they were very, very far, farther than the heath, farther than the land of firs and pine trees. They were at the shores of the great sea, in the land of the snakes, where the daughter of the blacksmith of Pont-de-Pîle ruled. In that land stood a tower with no roof or doors or windows, but with a well in the middle. The tower was a hundred fathoms high. The walls were made of stone so hard and mortar so tough that no pickaxe or explosive could break it. Only the Snake Queen had the power to enter and exit through a hole which always closed as soon as she had passed through.

The blacksmith of Pont-de-Pîle and the Snake Queen called the great eagles from the mountain. "Oh, great eagles from the mountain, listen well so that you will do each task as we command you. Take this good-for-nothing and carry him into the tower. He shall be a prisoner until he marries the Snake Queen. He shall sleep on the floor with the sky as his roof. When he is thirsty he may drink water from the well. But he shall never lack iron or silver or gold or diamonds or gemstones. You will bring me all his work. And when he has earned it a hundredfold, you shall cast him a crust of bread as black as a hearth and as bitter as bile."

The great eagles from the mountain obeyed. For seven years, the apprentice was alone in the tower. He slept on the ground with the sky as his roof. When he was thirsty he drank water from the well. He never lacked iron or silver or gold, nor diamonds or gemstones. The great eagles brought all his work to the blacksmith of Pont-de-Pîle. And when the apprentice had earned it a hundredfold, they cast him a crust of bread as black as a hearth and as bitter as bile.

Yet the apprentice did not always work for his master. Beneath his anvil he dug a deep hole, where he hid the things he forged for himself. The great eagles from the mountain never saw those.

First he forged an iron belt. The iron belt had three hooks.

Then he forged a pair of golden feet, which were as well shaped and fitted as his own feet which the blacksmith of Pont-de-Pile had sawn off and burnt.

Finally he forged a pair of large wings which were as light as a feather.

This work took him seven years.

Every evening at sunset, the Snake Queen came through the hole in the tower that opened only for her and closed as soon as she had passed through.

"Apprentice, your misfortune will come to an end as soon as I am your wife."

"Away with you, Snake Queen! I have a loved one. Never shall I take another."

They spoke so to each other every evening. But when everything was ready, the apprentice spoke differently.

"Apprentice, your misfortune will come to an end as soon as I am your wife."

"So come to me, Snake Queen. I shall deny my loved one. Never again will I think of her."

The Snake Queen lay on the ground next to the apprentice. They kissed each other and spoke of love until sunrise.

144

"Apprentice, your misfortune will end. Soon I will be your wife. Farewell. Tonight, at sunset, I shall return."

"Farewell, Snake Queen. I shall await you!"

That evening, one hour before sunset, the apprentice thought, *And now we shall laugh.*

He took his axe of fine steel, his broad and sharpened axe. He took out the iron belt, the iron belt with the three hooks. He fitted his golden feet. Then he pushed close to the wall and stood guard right by the hole through which the Snake Queen entered the tower every evening.

When the Snake Queen appeared, the apprentice quickly put his foot on her neck. She slithered and hissed but she could only bite his golden feet. With one strike of his axe, the apprentice severed her head and hung it from his iron belt. Then he put on his wings, which were as light as a feather, and he climbed to the highest point of the tower.

Night fell. The apprentice looked at the sky to find his way by the stars. Then he took to the air and flew a hundred times faster than a swallow.

Finally, he landed on the roof of the hospital of Lectoure, from where one could see the village of La Côte, the houses of Pont-de-Pîle and the River Gers. There he listened, and he watched, and he waited.

He heard the eleventh hour strike from all the towers of the town. Then he saw the blacksmith of Pont-de-Pîle step out of his house to turn into an otter and live in the lake until daybreak.

He waited until the last chime of midnight had passed. Then the apprentice flew a hundred times faster than a swallow to the hollowed willow where the blacksmith of Pont-de-Pîle hid his human skin every night. The skin soon hung from a hook on the iron belt, and the apprentice flew a hundred fathoms above the River Gers.

"Ho, blacksmith of Pont-de-Pîle. Ho! Ho!"

"What do you want, great bird?"

"Blacksmith of Pont-de-Pîle, I bring news from your daughter—news from the Snake Queen."

"Speak, great bird."

"I am no great bird. I am your apprentice. For seven years I suffered and died in a tower by the shores of the great sea. Blacksmith of Pont-de-Pîle, do you want news from your daughter—news from the Snake Queen? Listen! Your daughter now hangs from my belt in two pieces, head and body. Here, fish her out of the lake and see whether you can put her together again."

The blacksmith of Pont-de-Pîle screeched like an eagle.

"Blacksmith of Pont-de-Pîle, that shall not be your only misfortune. Search the hollowed willow for

146

your human skin. Search well, my friend. It hangs from my iron belt. And you shall be an otter for ever more."

The blacksmith of Pont-de-Pîle dived into the lake. He was never seen again.

Then the apprentice flew a hundred times faster than a swallow to his mother's hut.

Tap. Tap.

"Who is knocking?"

"Open up, Mother."

"Jesus and Mary! Is it you, my son? For seven years I have hoped for your return."

"Mother, I was not free to return before now. I am glad that the Good Lord and the Holy Virgin Mary have kept you well. Now, Mother, I shall be able to earn our keep. You will only work if you wish to. Without wanting to order you, Mother, light a fire, ready the skillet, put some bread on the table and a jug of wine with it. I bring the meat. It hangs from my belt."

"Jesus! My son! That is the skin of a Christian man."

"Mother, it is the skin of the blacksmith of Pont-de-Pîle. He was not a Christian. You will never see him again."

An hour later, the skin had been roasted and eaten.

"And now, blacksmith of Pont-de-Pîle, try to get your skin out of my belly."

Then the apprentice put on his wings, which were

as light as a feather, and he flew off a hundred times faster than a swallow.

Within five minutes, he stood by the chapel of Lagarde, where his loved one was sleeping in her grave. He pushed the door open and lit a candle by the light that burnt in honour of the holy sacraments. He lifted the stone from the grave vault as if it were as light as a cork, and he tore the lid from the casket.

"Ho, little maiden. Get up! You've been sleeping for seven years."

"Is that you, beautiful apprentice? So the misfortune no longer darkens your life. Look! I have done as you commanded. I am wearing my wedding dress, with the veil and the wreath of orange blossoms on my head, and the white roses on my belt."

"Get up, little maiden."

The little maiden got up. The apprentice carried her into the chapel, where both prayed to God for a long time.

"Little maiden, it is now day. Go to your chamber and stay there until I call for you."

"Beautiful apprentice, I shall obey you."

The little maiden went to her chamber.

And the apprentice went to the master and the mistress of the castle. "Good day, Marquis and Marquise of Fimarcon. Do you recognize me?"

"No, dear friend, we do not recognize you."

"That is not right. I am the apprentice of the black-smith of Pont-de-Pîle. Seven years ago I lived and worked here for two months, when your eldest daughter was wed to the King of the Sea Isles."

"You speak the truth, apprentice. Now we recognize you."

"Marquis and Marquise of Fimarcon, you had a youngest daughter, a little maiden of thirteen years. Is she now married to a prince?"

"Apprentice, our youngest daughter is in heaven. Seven years ago our Lord took her from us. We buried her as she requested, in a wedding dress, with a veil and a wreath of orange blossoms on her head, and white roses on her belt."

"Marquis and Marquise of Fimarcon, swear to me by your soul and upon pain of eternal damnation that you will give me your youngest daughter as a bride if I bring her to you alive."

"By our souls and upon pain of eternal damnation!"

"Marquis and Marquise of Fimarcon, quickly call the priest. I will bring you your daughter."

The apprentice brought in the little maiden. They were wed that same day, and the wedding lasted fourteen days. The apprentice and his wife lived a long and happy life, and they had twelve sons. The eldest was the strongest and fairest of them all. But his skin was covered in fine hairs that were as soft and brown as the fur of an otter. That was because on his wedding day his father had eaten the roasted skin of the blacksmith of Pont-de-Pile.

Of all the stories I chose for this book, Golden Foot *resonates loudest in* Reckless. *In fact, I made the young apprentice a character in* Living Shadows. *The richness of this tale enchanted me from the beginning. It was a wonderful find, and once again my visual imagination was triggered by the images: the boy who forges his own feet and wings to escape his evil master. The bride who sleeps for seven years in her coffin, with orange blossoms in her hair… and the eldest son who is born to the lovers with otter fur.*

One senses an older story underneath the Christian icing, from pagan times when people still shifted shape and turned into animals. It may have been the influence of the Christian faith that meant the shape-shifters are evil while the boy who engineers his own wings is the good and fearless hero. Or that the snake, once a sacred animal for the Greeks and in many other cultures, is shown as a treacherous seductress. Many tales give us this impression: that much of the imagery and symbolism originates from older stories, although their meaning is by now mysterious and misunderstood. But still they hold so much truth about human nature or a past that defines us that they continue to cast a spell even though they were forced into new Christian clothes and were altered to deliver a message that vilifies the pagan ideas that enchant us.

The
Story of One
Who Set Out
to Study Fear

father had two sons of whom the eldest was sensible and clever and good at everything but the youngest was stupid and could not understand or learn anything. People would look at him and say, "That one is going to give his father nothing but trouble." Now when there was anything to be done, it was the eldest who always had to do it, but if the father wanted something brought and it was already late, perhaps even night-time, and the way led through the churchyard or some other eerie place, he would say, "Oh, Father, no! I'm not going, it makes my flesh creep!" because he was afraid. Or, evenings, in front of the fire, when they told stories that make shivers run down your spine, the listeners would say, "Doesn't that make your flesh creep?" The youngest sat in his corner and listened too and could never understand what they meant. "They're always saying, 'It makes my flesh creep! It makes my flesh creep!' It doesn't make *my* flesh creep. This must be another skill I don't understand anything about."

Now one day it happened that the father said to him, "Listen, you over there in the corner! You're growing big and strong and you too will have to learn something with which to earn a living. Look at your brother, he always tries to do his best, but as for you! It's a waste of breath even talking to you!" "Oh, but Father," answered the boy, "there is something I would really like to learn. What I would like to learn, if possible, is how to make my flesh creep. That's something I don't understand anything about yet." The eldest son laughed when he heard this, and thought, "Good Lord, what a fathead my brother is! He'll never amount to anything as long as he lives. What would become a hook must crook itself be times." The father sighed and answered, "Your flesh will creep soon enough, but that'll never earn you a living."

Soon after this, the sexton came to call and the father told him about the trouble he was having with his youngest son, how useless he was, that he knew nothing and was going to learn nothing. "Just think, when I asked him how he was going to earn his living, he wanted, of all things, to learn how to make his flesh creep!" "If that's all he wants," answered the sexton, "there's something he can learn at my house. Let him come and live with me, I'll soon shape him up." The father was content, because he thought: "At least it will take some of the rough edges off the boy." And so the sexton took the boy into his house and his job was to ring the bell. After a few days, the sexton woke him around midnight and told him to get up, climb into the church tower, and toll the bell. "You're going to learn what it's like when your flesh creeps," he thought, and secretly went ahead; when the boy came up and turned around to take hold of the bell rope, there, standing on the stair opposite the louvres, he saw a white shape. "Who goes there?" he called, but the shape gave no answer, stood and never stirred. "Answer me," called the boy, "or get out! You've got no business here at night." But the sexton kept standing there, motionless, to make the boy think it was a ghost. And for the second time the boy called, "What are you doing here? Speak up, if you're a true man, or I'll throw you down the stairs." The sexton thought, "He doesn't really mean it," didn't make a sound and stood as if he were made of stone. So the boy called out for the third time and when that did no good he took a run and pushed the ghost down the stairs, so that it fell ten steps and remained lying in a corner. Thereupon he tolled the bell and went home, lay down in his bed without a word and went back to sleep. The sexton's wife waited for her husband a long time, but he didn't and didn't come back. In the end she got worried, woke the boy up and asked, "You don't know what happened to my husband, do you? He climbed into the tower ahead of you." "No," answered the boy, "but there was somebody standing on the stair opposite the louvres and when he didn't answer me and wouldn't go away either, I took him for some rascal and pushed him downstairs. Why don't you go over and then you'll see if it was your husband, and if it was I'm very sorry." Off ran the woman and found her husband lying in a corner, whimpering, and he had a broken leg.

She carried him down and then she ran to the boy's father screaming and hollering. "Your boy," she cried, "has caused a great tragedy. He threw my husband down the stairs, so that he broke a leg. Get this good-for-nothing out of our house." The father was horror-stricken and came running and scolded the boy. "What kind of wicked trick is this! The devil himself must have put you up to it." "But, Father," answered he, "just listen to me, will you! I didn't do anything wrong. There he stood in the night, and looked like he was up to no good. I didn't know who it was and I warned him three times to speak up or go away." "Ah," said the father, "with you I will have nothing but grief. Go on! Get out of my sight, I don't want to look at you any more." "Oh, all right, Father, that's fine by me, just wait till daylight, and then I'll go away and learn to make my flesh creep, so that at least I'll have some skill with which to earn my living." "Learn what you want," said the father, "it's all the same to me. Here are fifty thalers, take them and go out into the wide world and don't tell anybody where you come from or who your father is, because I am ashamed of you." "Right you are, Father. Whatever you say. If that's what you want, I can do that."

Now, at daybreak the boy put his fifty thalers in his pocket and walked out onto the great highway, mumbling to himself, "If I could only make my flesh creep! Oh, if my flesh would only creep!" A man walking along behind him heard this conversation the boy was having with himself and when they had walked awhile, and come within sight of the gallows, the man said, "Look, there's the tree on which seven have had their wedding with the ropemaker's daughter and are learning how to fly. Go sit underneath, wait till night comes and it will make your flesh creep all right." "If that's all there is to it," answered the boy, "it's easy. If my flesh really learns to creep as fast as that, you can have my fifty thalers. Come back and see me in the morning." So the boy walked over to the gallows, sat down underneath, and waited till evening, and because he was cold, he made a fire. But around midnight the wind blew so bitterly he could not keep warm, and as the wind set the hanged men moving to and fro and knocked one against the other, he thought: "You're freezing down here by your fire, no wonder they are freezing and fidgeting up there." And because he had a kind heart, he got the ladder, climbed up, untied one after the other, and brought all seven of them down. Then he stoked the fire, blew on it, and set them around it so they might warm themselves. But they sat and didn't stir, and the fire caught their clothes, so he said, "Take care, or I'll string you up again." But the dead men didn't hear, said nothing, and let their rags go on burning, and so he became annoyed and said, "If you won't take care of yourselves, I can't help you. I don't want to burn to a cinder along with you," and strung them up again, one after the other. Now he sat down by his fire and went to sleep and next morning the man came and wanted his fifty thalers and said, "Now do you know what it's like to feel your flesh creep?" "No," answered he. "How am I supposed to know? Those characters up there never opened their mouths and were so stupid they let the few old rags they have on their bodies catch fire." So the man saw he wasn't going to collect any fifty thalers that day, and went away saying, "I never met one like that before."

The boy too went on his way and started talking to himself again. "Oh, if I could only make my flesh creep! Oh, if my flesh would only creep!" A wagoner who was striding along behind him heard and asked, "Who are you?" "I don't know," answered the boy. The wagoner went on questioning him: "Where are you from?" "I don't know." "Who is your father?" "I mustn't tell." "What's that you keep muttering between your teeth?" "Oh," answered the boy, "I want my flesh to creep, but no one can teach me how." "Stop babbling," said the wagoner. "Come with me and I'll see if I can't find you a place with a good master somewhere." So the boy went along with the wagoner and in the evening they came to an inn where they could spend the night, and as they entered the room the boy began again very loudly: "If I could only make my flesh creep. If my flesh would only creep." The innkeeper heard him, laughed, and said, "If that's what you need to make you happy, there's a great opportunity for you right here." "Oh, be quiet," said the innkeeper's wife. "There's a lot of smart alecks have already paid with their lives, and wouldn't it be a shame if these pretty eyes never saw the light of day again?" But the boy said, "Let it be ever so hard, I want to learn it once and for all. That's what I set out to study." He left the innkeeper no peace until he told him that not far away there stood an enchanted castle where a man could certainly learn what it's like when your flesh creeps by just going up and watching for three nights, and that the king had promised his daughter's hand to anyone who dared, and she was the most beautiful girl under the sun; and that there was a great treasure in the castle, guarded by evil spirits, and then it would be freed and there was enough to make any poor man rich. Many's the one who had gone in, but no one had come out again. And so the next morning the boy went to the king and said, "If you please, I would like to watch in the enchanted castle for three nights." The king looked at the boy and because he liked him he said, "You may ask for any three things, so long as they're not live, to take into the castle with you." And so the boy answered, "Well, then I want fire, and a lathe, and a bench with a vise and the whittling knife that goes with it."

The king had everything carried into the castle while it was still daylight, and when night was drawing in, the boy went up, made himself a bright fire in one of the rooms, put up the bench with the knife beside it, and sat down on the lathe. "If I could only make my flesh creep," he said, "but I'm never going to learn it here!" Towards midnight he went to stoke his fire and as he was blowing on it there suddenly came a screeching out of the corners. "Ow, miaow, how cold we are!" "You fools," he called out, "what are you screaming about? If you're cold, come and sit by the fire and warm yourselves." No sooner had he spoken than two big black cats came out with a mighty leap, sat down on either side, and looked at him ferociously with their fiery eyes. After a while, when they had warmed themselves, they said, "Friend, how about a little hand of cards?" "Why not?" answered he. "But first show me your paws." And so they stretched out their claws. "My," said he, "don't you have long nails! Wait, first I've got to trim them for you." And so he took them by the scruff of the neck, lifted them onto his bench, and screwed their paws fast. "One look at your fingers," said he, "and I've lost my yen for any hand of cards with you," and then he killed them and threw them into the water outside. No sooner had he made an end of those two and was about to sit down by his fire than out of every nook and cranny there came black cats and black dogs on smouldering chains, always more and more, until there was not one safe spot for him to stand. They screamed abominably, climbed all over his fire, tore it up and tried to put it out. For a while he watched quietly, but then it got too much for him, and he took his whittling knife and cried, "Away with you, scum!" and started to hit at them. Some ran away, the others he killed and threw out into the pond, and when he came back, he blew a fresh fire from the embers and warmed himself. And as he sat there, his eyes would not stay open and he felt like going to sleep, and so he looked around and saw a big bed in a corner. "Just what I need," said he, and went and lay down in it, but just as he was going to close his eyes, the bed began to ride away of its own accord and rode all over the whole castle. "That's all right by me," he said. "But can't you go a bit faster, please?" The bed rolled along as if it had six horses in harness, over the threshold, upstairs and down. All of a sudden, *crash bang*, it turned over and lay upside down on top of him like a mountain, but he tossed covers and pillows into the air, climbed out, and said, "Now let someone else take a ride," and lay down by his fire and slept till daybreak. In the morning the king came, and when he saw him lying there on the ground, he thought the spirits had taken his life and that he was dead, and so he said, "What a pity for this beautiful young man." The boy heard him, sat up, and said, "It hasn't come to that yet," and the king was amazed but very pleased and asked him how he had got on. "Pretty well," answered he. "One night has passed and so will the two others." When he came back to the inn, the innkeeper stared at him wide-eyed. "I didn't think," said he, "that I'd ever see you alive again. Now have you learnt what it's like to have your flesh creep?" "No," he said. "There's no help for me. If only someone could explain it to me."

The second night he went back into the old castle, sat down by the fire, and started up his old song: "If my flesh would only creep!" As midnight approached, one could hear a rumbling and a clattering, first softly, then stronger and stronger. Then it was quiet for a bit. At last, with a loud screech, half of a man came down the chimney and fell right in front of him. "Hey there!" cried he, "there's a half missing. This is not enough." And so the din started all over again: there was a heaving and a howling and out fell the other half as well. "Wait," said he, "first let me make up the fire a little for you." When he had done so, he looked around again and the two halves had joined together and there, in his place on the lathe, sat a grisly man. "That was not part of the bargain," said the boy. "That's my seat." The man tried to shove him away but the boy would not give in and pushed him off by force and sat down again in his own place. And so then still more men kept falling out, one after the other, and they brought nine dead men's bones and two skulls, set up a game of ninepins, and began to play. The boy felt like playing too, and said, "Listen, can I play?" "Yes, if you have money." "Plenty of money," answered he, "but your bowls are not quite round." And so he took the skulls, put them in his lathe, and turned them until they were round. "There. Now they'll roll better," he said. "Hey, this is fun!" He played with them and lost a little money, but when midnight tolled, everything disappeared in front of his eyes. He lay down and went quietly to sleep. The next morning came the king to enquire after him. "How did it go this time?" he asked. "I played at ninepins," answered he, "and lost a couple of pennies." "And it didn't make your flesh creep?" "Heavens no," said he, "I had a good time. Oh, if I only knew what it feels like to have one's flesh creep!"

On the third night he sat down again on his lathe and said crossly, "If my flesh would only *creep*." When it was quite late, six tall men came carrying a coffin. The boy said, "Aha! That must be my cousin who died a couple of days ago," beckoned with his finger and cried, "Come in, cousin, come along in." They set the coffin down on the floor and he went over and took the lid off. There was a dead man lying inside. He touched his face and it was cold as ice. "Wait," said he, "I'll warm you up a little," went to the fire, warmed his hand, and laid it against the dead man's face, but he remained cold, and so he took him out, sat down in front of the fire, and laid him on his lap and rubbed his arms to set the blood in motion. When that did no good either, it came to him that when two lie in bed together they warm each other up, so he put him in the bed, lay down beside him, and pulled up the covers. And after a little while the dead man did warm up and began to stir, and the boy said, "There, you see, cousin? I warmed you up, didn't I?" But the dead man lifted his voice and cried, "Now I will strangle you!" "What," said he, "is this the thanks I get? You're going right back in your coffin," picked him up, threw him in, and closed the lid; then the six men came and carried him away. "My flesh will not and will not creep," said he, "I'll never learn it here as long as I live."

Then there entered a man who was bigger than all the rest, and looked horrible and old, with a long white beard. "Wretch!" cried he. "Now you shall learn how it feels to have your flesh creep—you are going to die." "Not so fast," answered the boy. "If I'm the one to do the dying, I have to be there, don't I?" "I'll catch you yet," said the monster. "Take it easy, now," said the boy. "You talk big, but I'm as strong as you are and probably stronger." "That remains to be seen," said the old man. "If you are stronger, I will let you go. Come, we'll put it to the test." And so he led him along dark passages to a blacksmith's forge, took an axe, and with one blow drove the anvil into the ground. "I can do better than that," said the boy, and walked over to the other anvil. The old man came and stood next to him to watch, and his white beard hung down. And so the boy took hold of the axe and with one blow split the anvil in two and caught the old man's beard in the middle. "Now I've got you," said the boy, "and it's you who's going to die." And he picked up an iron bar and began to beat the old man until he whimpered and begged him to stop and promised to give him great riches. The boy pulled out the axe and let him go. The old man led him back to the castle and showed him a cellar with three chests full of gold. "Of these," said he, "one part is for the poor, another belongs to the king, the third is yours." With that, midnight struck, the spirit disappeared, and there stood the boy in the dark. "I'll get myself out of here," said he, groped around, found the way into the room with the fire, and fell asleep. The next morning came the king and said, "Now you must have learnt what it is to have your flesh creep." "No," said he. "Whatever can it be? My dead cousin was here, and a man with a beard came and showed me a lot of money, but nobody said a word about creeping flesh." The king said, "You have set the castle free and shall marry my daughter." "That's all very well," answered he, "but I still don't know a thing about getting my flesh to creep."

And so the gold was brought up and the wedding celebrated, but the young king, dearly though he loved his wife, and happy though he was, still kept saying, "If I could only make my flesh creep, oh, if my flesh would only creep," until the queen got angry. Her maid said, "I know what to do. His flesh is going to learn all about creeping." She went out to the brook that flowed through the garden and had them bring her a bucket full of minnows. At night, when the young king was asleep, his wife had to pull off the covers and pour the bucketful of cold water and the minnows on him. The little fish squirmed all over him, and he woke up and cried, "Something is making my flesh creep! Dear wife, how my flesh is creeping! Ah, now I know what it's like when one's flesh creeps."

I have always loved this tale and its strange and fearless hero. Of all the princes and adventurous rascals the fairy tales of my native country offer, I guess I would choose him as my king. Though he would have to get better with frogs.

The Frog
Princess

ong ago, when magic still roamed the hills and strange things happened, there lived a great king and queen with their three sons. These sons were their parents' pride and joy, and each day they grew taller, stronger and more handsome. One day the king called them together and said, "My sons, my falcons, you are now grown men. It is time that you married. Shoot an arrow into the sky and where it lands you will find your bride."

With hearts surging, the young men ran for their bows and arrows, and then took turns shooting. The oldest son was first. *Zing!* His arrow soared high, high above the clouds, and finally dropped to the ground in a neighbouring kingdom. The young man jumped on his horse and galloped off to find the arrow.

The arrow landed in a garden where a beautiful princess was strolling. Seeing something strange fall from the sky, the princess ran to see what it was. A delicate silver arrow lay among the roses. The princess picked it up and ran to find her father.

"Look, *Tato*, a silver arrow fell from the sky into our garden," she said.

Her father nodded wisely. "Ah, it's an omen. Save it for the one who will marry you."

When the prince arrived at the garden, he saw the lovely maiden with his arrow in her hand. He strode boldly up to her, saying, "I believe that's my arrow."

But the princess clutched the arrow to her breast. "The only one who can take it from me is he who will marry me," she replied.

"I will marry you," said the prince. And so they were engaged.

When the second son shot his arrow, *swoosh*, it flew over the treetops, just beneath the clouds, and landed in the courtyard of a wealthy merchant. The second son jumped on his horse and galloped off to find his arrow.

His arrow landed at the feet of the merchant's beautiful daughter, who sat on the steps fanning herself. When she saw the arrow, she immediately reached for it. "Ah, pretty," she said, marvelling at its delicacy. Then she took the arrow to her father and said, "Look what fell from the sky, father."

"It's a sign," said the merchant, "save it for the man who will marry you." The girl smiled and went skipping out to the courtyard. Just then the prince arrived and dismounted from his horse. He walked up to the maiden.

"That's my arrow," he said to the young woman, and he reached out for it. But the girl's fingers tightened around the arrow as she replied, "It belongs only to the man who will marry me."

"I will marry you," was the prince's answer. And so they were engaged.

Then the third son, whose name was Vasyl', shot his arrow. *Twang!* It spun around, zigzagged through the forest and flew into a swamp. Vasyl' shrugged, jumped on his horse and galloped off to find the arrow.

Now, it happened that there was a frog sitting on a lily pad in the middle of the swamp. As the arrow whizzed by, out went the frog's tongue to catch it. Seeing that this was not a dragonfly or anything else a frog could eat, she dropped it to the lily pad and placed two of her green, webbed feet over it. There she sat with her eyes bulging, smiling a strange frog smile, until the prince arrived. When Vasyl' saw his arrow on the lily pad, he waded through the swamp to get it, thinking, "What a bad shot! My next try will be better." But when he reached for the arrow, much to his surprise, the frog spoke.

"I will only give it to the one who marries me."

What? Vasyl' couldn't believe his ears. His head began to reel, but he picked up the frog and his arrow, put them in his pocket, and turned homeward. When he reached the castle, he saw that his two older brothers were already there. Each had a fine maiden on his arm and when Vasyl' saw this, he hung his head in shame.

"What is it, son?" asked the king.

Vasyl' pulled the frog from his pocket and said, "Both of my brothers have found beautiful wives, but my arrow landed in the swamp and was snatched up by this wretched frog."

"Marry her," said the father, "for it is your fate."

So the king and queen held a triple wedding for their sons. The eldest walked proudly down the aisle with a beautiful princess on his arm. Behind him walked the second son with the merchant's lovely daughter on his arm. Last came Vasyl'. He walked down the aisle with a little satin pillow, upon which sat, well, a slimy green frog.

The king and queen gave each couple a home as a wedding gift, and peace, if not happiness, reigned in each household. Then one day the royal couple decided to get to know their new daughters-in-law. They called their sons together and said, "Let's see if your wives can spin and weave. Ask them to make us a piece of cloth."

When Vasyl' heard this, his heart sank. The two oldest sons hurried to their wives with the royal request, but Vasyl' stumbled home slowly and then sat by the fire weeping.

"What is it, my husband? Why do you cry?" the frog asked.

"Mother and Father want each of the new wives to weave a piece of fine cloth. How can I ask you to do this? You cannot weave. You have webbed feet—why, you're just a frog." Vasyl' began sobbing again.

"Don't fret, Vasyl'. Let's see what tomorrow brings." Vasyl' stopped crying, for he really had no choice, and went to bed. As soon as his head hit the pillow and his eyes fluttered shut, something strange happened. The frog rose on two legs, stepped out of her frog skin, and became a young maiden.

She whistled and a loom appeared. She snapped her fingers and piles of coloured yarns and threads took shape. She clapped her hands and a dozen maids gathered together and began working. All night they worked together. They spun, they wove, they measured, they cut, they sewed and they embroidered. By the time the dawn came, they had woven two beautiful shirts of the finest linen, embroidered with many bright colours. The frog wife quietly laid the shirts next to her husband's pillow and climbed back into her frog skin.

When Vasyl' awoke, he was truly amazed. Never had he seen such beautiful garments. He took the shirts to the king and queen, presenting them with a bow.

"I have never seen such exquisite handiwork," marvelled the queen. The king too exclaimed and he put his shirt on, beaming.

"Your wife has done well," said the king. "Your older brothers' wives gave us only handkerchiefs." The queen shook her head sadly.

Vasyl' smiled, but his smile vanished like smoke with his father's next request.

"Now let's see how our new daughters-in-law can cook. We'll have the wives each bake a sweet treat for us and bring it to the castle tomorrow."

Again, the two older sons ran to their wives quickly, but Vasyl' dragged himself home slowly, stumbling and sighing. He sat on the stoop with his head in his hands until the frog came out and spoke to him.

"What now, dear?" her soft voice interrupted his thoughts.

"Father and mother want to find out which of their daughters-in-law is the best cook. How can you, a frog who eats nothing but mosquitoes and flies, cook for the king and queen?" Vasyl' shook his head sadly, but once again the frog comforted him.

"Oh, please don't worry, my husband. Let's see what tomorrow brings." Vasyl' took his wife's words to heart and went to bed.

Again the frog stepped out of her skin, whistled, snapped her fingers, and clapped her hands. Again the night maidens came, this time with buckets of cream, baskets of fresh eggs, flour as light as fairy dust, creamy butter, and the finest sugar. All night the maidens toiled. They stirred, they measured, they mixed, they poured and they baked. By morning there stood a cake as tall as the king himself, decorated with little doves, pine cones and garlands of periwinkle. The frog wife set it next to her husband's pillow and tiptoed away to find her frog skin.

When Vasyl' awoke, he gasped with delight. This was a cake like none he had ever seen. He carried it off to the palace, and the king and queen made no end of their praises. As for the sweets from the other daughters, well, the burnt *kalach* (that is, buns) and soggy *varenyky* (dumplings) were thrown to the dogs— and even the dogs turned up their noses and walked away.

Vasyl' was beginning to realize that his frog wife had talents, but just as his pride began to swell, his parents made a third request that crushed his heart.

"In honour of our sons and their wives, we are planning a royal dinner," said the queen. "We'll invite everyone in the kingdom to feast and dance with us. You and your wife will have the seats of honour, Vasyl'."

Vasyl' imagined how ashamed he would be, sitting in the seat of honour next to his frog wife. How people would laugh, especially when she ate! And when they danced? Oh, it was too much to bear.

Disheartened, Vasyl' returned home, where once again he hung his head and cried.

"What's troubling you today, Vasyl'? Didn't your parents like my cake?" asked the frog.

Vasyl' explained what had happened, and the frog gave her usual answer: "Don't worry, let's see what tomorrow brings."

Vasyl' slept well, but the next day, as he prepared for the feast, he became sadder and sadder. Seeing her husband's grief, the frog spoke.

"You go ahead to the party," she said. "When it begins to rain, you'll know I am bathing. When the lightning flashes, I will be dressing myself in the finest garments. And when the thunder cracks, my carriage will arrive at your father's castle."

Well, what could Vasyl' do? He did as his wife told him, but when he arrived at the palace, his brothers and their wives began poking fun at him.

"Where's your frog?" teased the oldest brother.

"Ribbet, ribbet (or, as frogs say in Ukraine, *kvak, kvak*)," mocked the second brother. Their wives tittered and blushed.

Now guests from all over the kingdom began arriving. When everyone was seated at the long banquet table, it began to rain.

"That is my wife washing herself," announced Vasyl'.

The room grew quiet as everyone stared in amazement. The brothers and their wives looked at one another and rolled their eyes. The lightning flashed.

"And that is my wife dressing herself," said Vasyl'. Now the crowd began to whisper, and the brothers and their wives glanced at Vasyl' as though he had just taken leave of his senses. The thunder cracked.

"Ah, that will be my wife arriving," said Vasyl'. He stood up just as she entered—the most beautiful woman anyone had ever seen, draped in a golden gown embroidered with all the colours of the rainbow. Everyone gasped as she glided to the table and took her seat beside Vasyl'. Could this be the frog that the brothers had been joking about earlier?

As for Vasyl'—well, Vasyl' could not take his eyes off this lovely creature. He simply could not believe what he was seeing.

When the food was served, everyone fell to eating, and so did the princes and their wives. But as beautiful as she was, Vasyl' 's wife had strange table manners. She ate a piece of chicken and tucked the bones in her right sleeve. She took a sip of wine and then poured the rest down her left sleeve. The two other daughters-in-law noticed this and whispered between themselves. They did not want to be outdone by a frog again, so they did the same as she had done.

When everyone had finished eating, the musicians began to play. The king turned to his sons, saying, "You lead the dance with your wives!"

But the wives of the two older brothers backed away. "Let Vasyl' and his wife dance first," they said. As Vasyl' and his wife stepped out on the dance floor, they watched closely, hoping to mimic the frog-woman's every move.

The princess was as graceful as she was beautiful. Her tiny feet barely touched the ground as she and her husband swirled over the floor. Holding her close, Vasyl' stared rapturously at his wife. Could this really be the same frog he had married? Soon he told his wife that he was tired of dancing and sneaked away to wonder at his fate.

Now the princess danced alone, spinning and swaying with such grace that the crowd was hypnotized. She waved her right arm and a shimmering pond appeared. Then the princess waved her left arm and snowy swans glided upon the pond. Tiny stars fell from the sky to float on the placid water. Everyone gasped in amazement. Finally the princess took her seat.

"Bravo! Bravo!" bellowed the king. The queen clapped vigorously and beamed with joy.

Then the wives of the older brothers ran out to the floor and began dancing. They were so awkward that they tripped over their own feet, and people in the crowd turned away in embarrassment for the young women. Desperate for attention, the women began mimicking the beautiful princess. They waved their right arms and greasy bones tumbled from their sleeves. They waved their left arms and wine drops flew out, spattering right in the king's face. "Enough, you clumsy fools," he roared. "We'll all dance now."

So everyone from the king to the cook crowded into the courtyard and began dancing. Everyone, that is, except Vasyl'. He was hurrying home to solve the mystery of his wife's newfound beauty.

When Vasyl' reached the house, he immediately understood what had happened, for there in the middle of the floor lay a crumpled frog skin. "Never again will my beautiful wife be seen as a frog," he said to himself. With that he seized the skin and threw it in the fire, where it hissed and sputtered and burnt. When Vasyl' was certain the skin had burnt to ashes, he returned to the party, joyous at last.

All night long the people feasted and danced. Everyone was happy, from the poorest peasant to the king himself, and only when dawn peeked over the horizon did the guests depart from the great palace.

With their arms and hearts entwined, Vasyl' and his princess returned home. Vasyl' immediately climbed into bed, but the princess began searching for her frog skin.

"Have you seen my garment?" she called to Vasyl'.

"What? That ugly old frog skin? I threw it in the fire so you'd never have to wear it again," Vasyl' boasted. But the princess burst into tears.

"Oh, my Vasyl', you should not have touched it! My father has put a spell on me and without the frog skin, I cannot stay. Now I must leave for the crystal kingdom. Goodbye, my dear husband." As she spoke, the princess turned into a cuckoo bird, flew out the window, and disappeared, leaving Vasyl' alone in his misery.

For several days the young prince moped about, hoping his wife would return and wondering what to do. Every time a bird flew by or called out from a treetop, Vasyl' chased after it, but it was no use. When his grief became too heavy to bear, he packed his bow and arrows and set off in search of his beloved princess.

Vasyl' walked and walked. He trudged through a dark wood, he crossed a churning river and he kept walking. He passed through many lands he did not know, but he asked everyone he met about the crystal kingdom. Not one person had even heard of it.

Then one day Vasyl' came upon a shrivelled old man, so old that his skin was white as snow and his white hair and beard nearly reached the ground.

"Good day, my friend, and what brings you here?" greeted the old man.

"I'm going to the crystal kingdom to seek my wife," replied Vasyl'. "Can you tell me how to get there from here?"

The old man nodded solemnly. "I can tell you, but you'll never make it, son."

His heart leapt at the old man's words. "You must tell me, sir, for if I don't find my wife, I will surely die of loneliness."

A sad smile came over the old man's face as he handed Vasyl' a red ball of string. "Throw this ball of string before you," he said, "and follow it wherever it goes."

Vasyl' took the ball eagerly and rolled it before him. It led him into a forest so thick that no light could be seen—it was black as night. Two eyes shone in the dark and Vasyl' thought he felt the hot breath of a bear at his back. Fear seized his heart. Quickly he grabbed his bow and arrow. He was about to shoot when the bear spoke.

"Don't kill me, kind prince. I will be a friend to you someday." So Vasyl' put away his bow and arrow and went on his way. When he came to the edge of the forest, he heard the flap of great wings and the shriek of a large bird. Looking up, Vasyl' saw a majestic falcon sitting at the top of a tall pine, glaring down at him. Again Vasyl' reached for his bow and arrow. He was about to shoot when the falcon spoke.

"Don't kill me, kind prince. I will be a friend to you someday." Again Vasyl' put his bow and arrow away and continued his journey. Then he came to the edge of a sea and saw a large pike lying on the shore, gasping for air.

"This might make me a fine dinner," Vasyl' said to himself, as he reached for his bow and arrow. But once again, he stopped as words came from the pike's gaping mouth.

"Do not kill me, friend," said the pike, "for I can be of service to you someday." Once again Vasyl' put his weapons away. He threw the fish back into the sea and walked on.

After many days, Vasyl' reached the end of the string. He saw no crystal kingdom and no princess. The only thing he saw was a meagre hut with foul-smelling smoke belching from its chimney. Vasyl' didn't know what to do, so he stepped up to the door and knocked.

"Who's there?" shrieked a voice from inside. Before Vasyl' could answer, the door swung open and there stood the oldest, ugliest woman he had ever seen. *Baba Yaha* stood about three feet high on crooked stick-legs. Her skin was yellow, covered with knobby warts, and her thin hair hung in mats over a misshapen head. Her beady red eyes darted quickly over Vasyl' and then she smiled a toothless grin.

"What have we here? Could it be a handsome young prince paying me a call?" she said coyly, and then her face twisted into a hateful grimace. "What brings you here, lad? Are you hiding from someone or seeking someone? Answer me!"

"I'm seeking my beloved wife, the frog," Vasyl' answered earnestly. The old woman cackled and clapped her gnarled hands.

"You will never find her now," she taunted. "She belongs to my brother, the dragon in the crystal kingdom, and if he sets eyes on the likes of you, you're bound to be his dinner."

But Vasyl' was not deterred. "Please, grandmother, tell me how to get there."

The old hag smiled and her heart softened at the prince's sincerity. "The crystal kingdom is on an island in the middle of the sea. My brother lives in a great palace and it is there you will find your wife—*if* you ever get there, that is. No one in their right mind would even try to go to such a dangerous place. Everyone knows my brother is merciless. If he even so much as sees you, you will surely die." The old woman cackled again.

Vasyl' thanked the hag and retraced his steps to the sea. As he approached, he became dismayed. The sea was huge and he could barely even see the island. How would he ever get there? Vasyl' looked about for something to use as a raft, but the shoreline was empty. Suddenly a great splash interrupted his search. It was the pike.

"What troubles you, prince?" asked the fish.

"I must get to the crystal kingdom, but I haven't a way to cross the water," Vasyl' moaned.

"Don't worry—I'll help you," said the pike. He slapped his great tail against the water and up rose a shining bridge leading straight to the island. Vasyl' thanked the pike and hurried across the bridge.

When he reached the island, though, he saw that the castle was surrounded by a forest so thick he could not pass through the trees. Vasyl' tried to pry apart the thick branches, but he was weak with hunger. He sat down on a mossy rock and his eyes filled with tears. He had come all this way and now he would surely die of starvation.

Just then a rabbit hopped across his path and from out of the clouds swooped the falcon. The great bird pounced on the rabbit, carried it to Vasyl', and dropped it at the prince's feet. Vasyl' built a fire, cooked the rabbit, and ate it. Feeling better, he started towards the woods again, thinking, "There must be a way to get through it." Just then, the bear appeared.

"My friend, what brings you to this strange land?" asked the bear.

"My wife is held captive at the crystal kingdom," Vasyl' replied. "I want to free her, but I can't get through these woods."

The bear tossed his head to the side and roared. "I can help with that," he said. He put his huge arms around a tree, grunted, and pulled it out, roots and all. Then he pulled another out, and another, until there was a clear path leading straight to the castle. Vasyl' thanked the bear and hurried down the path. By the time he reached the palace, he was weak and panting, but he pushed on the heavy gate and stepped through it. The gate slammed shut behind him.

When he entered the castle, all Vasyl' saw was winding halls lined with glass. He slipped up one hallway and down another, peeking in each door but seeing only his reflection in the glass walls. Deeper and deeper into the crystal kingdom he ventured. All the while he listened for the dragon and for the voice of his wife, but all he heard was the echo of his own footsteps. Finally he reached the heart of the castle, where there was one last door to open. Was that the faint sobbing of a woman he heard? Vasyl' held his breath and his hand trembled as he touched the door. As the door swung open, Vasyl' saw his wife. She sat spinning as though in a trance, pale and sorrowful. Still, she was more beautiful than ever.

"My beloved," Vasyl' spoke softly. The princess lifted her head and joy flooded the room like sunshine as they embraced.

"Because you have come for me, my father's spell is broken," she said. "Now we can be together."

Just then the heavy footsteps of the dragon thundered in the halls. The walls shone with the reflection of his fiery breath and the smell of smoke entered the room. The prince's heart pounded as he looked about, realizing that the gate had closed behind him and there was no place to hide!

"Hurry, my love," said the princess. As Vasyl' turned to her, she once again changed into a cuckoo. She took Vasyl' under her wing, flew up to the rafters and escaped through a small window. As they left the crystal kingdom, Vasyl' and the princess saw forests go up in the flames of the dragon's wrath.

The cuckoo and the prince flew through the heavens for many days. When they reached home, the princess changed back to her true, beautiful form. That is how she stayed with Vasyl' for the rest of their days.

Vasyl' and his wife lived long, happy lives. They had many handsome sons and lovely daughters and each was brighter than the next. But there was one strange thing about these children: more than anything else they all loved to play in the frog pond behind the castle!

This story is such an enchanting rival to the Frog Prince *tale I grew up with. The prince actually behaves better than the princess we meet in the German fairy tale because at least he doesn't throw his frog bride against a wall. And I love the strength and skilfulness of the Frog Princess. She definitely isn't a complainer like the Frog Prince in the Grimm's tale.*

The
One-Handed
Murderer

here was once a miser king, so miserly that he kept his only daughter in the garret for fear someone would ask for her hand and thus oblige him to provide her with a dowry.

One day a murderer came to town and stopped at the inn across the street from the king's palace. Right away he wanted to know who lived over there. "That's the home of a king," he was told, "so miserly that he keeps his daughter in the garret."

So what does the murderer do at night but climb up on the king's roof and open the small garret window. Lying in bed, the princess saw the window open and a man on the ledge. "Help! Burglar!" she screamed. The murderer closed the window and fled over the rooftops. The servants came running, saw the window closed, and said, "Your Highness, you were dreaming. There's no one here."

The next morning she asked her father to let her out of the garret, but the king said, "Your fears are imaginary. No one in the world would ever think of coming up here."

The second night the murderer opened the window at the same hour. "Help! Burglar!" screamed the princess, but again he got away, and no one would believe her.

The third night she fastened the window with a strong chain and, with pounding heart, stood guard all by herself, holding a knife. The murderer tried to open the window, but couldn't. He thrust in one hand, and the princess cut it clean off at the wrist. "You wretch!" cried the murderer. "You'll pay for that!" And he fled over the rooftops.

The princess showed the king and the court the amputated hand, and everybody finally believed her and complimented her courage. From that day on, she no longer slept in the garret.

Not too long after that, the king received a request for an audience from an elegant young stranger who wore gloves. He was so well-spoken that the king took an instant liking to him. Talking of this and that, the stranger mentioned that he was a bachelor in search of a genteel bride, whom he would marry without a dowry, being so wealthy himself. Hearing that, the king thought, "This is just the husband for my daughter", and he sent for her. The minute the princess saw the man she shuddered, having the strong impression she already knew him. Once she was alone with her father, she said, "Majesty, I'm all but sure that's the burglar whose hand I cut off."

"Nonsense," replied the king. "Didn't you notice his beautiful hands and elegant gloves? He's a nobleman, beyond any shadow of a doubt."

To make a long story short, the stranger asked for the princess's hand, and to obey her father and escape his tyranny, she said yes. The wedding was short and simple, since the bridegroom couldn't remain away from his business and the king was unwilling to spend any money. He gave his daughter, for a bridal present, a walnut necklace and a worn-out foxtail. Then the newlyweds drove off at once in a carriage.

The carriage entered a forest, but instead of following the main road it turned off onto a scarcely visible trail that led deeper and deeper into the underbrush. When they had gone some distance, the bridegroom said, "My dear, pull off my glove."

She did, and discovered a stump. "Help!" she cried, realizing she'd married the man whose hand she had cut off.

"You're in my power now," said the man. "I am a murderer by profession, mind you. I'll now get even with you for maiming me."

The murderer's house was at the edge of the forest, by the sea. "Here I've stored all the treasure of my victims," he said, pointing to the house, "and you will stay and guard it."

He chained her to a tree in front of the house and

197

walked off. The princess remained by herself, tethered like a dog, and before her was the sea, over which a ship glided from time to time. She tried signalling to a passing ship. On board they saw her through their telescope and sailed closer to see what the matter was. The crew disembarked, and she told them her story. So they set her free and took her aboard, together with all the murderer's treasure.

It was a ship of cotton merchants, who thought it wise to conceal the princess and all the treasure underneath the bales of cotton. The murderer returned and found his wife gone and the house ransacked. She could have only escaped by the sea, he thought to himself, and then saw the ship disappearing into the distance. He got into his swift sailboat and caught up with the ship. "All that cotton overboard!" he ordered. "I must find my wife, who has fled."

"Do you want to ruin us?" asked the merchants. "Why not run your sword through the bales to see if anyone is hiding in them?"

The murderer started piercing the cotton with his sword and, before long, wounded the girl hiding there. But as he drew his sword out, the cotton wiped the blood off, and the sword came out clean.

"Listen," said the sailors, "we saw another ship approach the coast, that one down there."

"I'll investigate at once," said the murderer. He left the ship carrying cotton and directed his sailboat towards the other ship.

The girl, who had received a mere scratch on her arm, was put ashore in a safe port. But she protested, saying, "Throw me into the sea! Throw me into the sea!"

The sailors talked the matter over, and one old-timer in their midst whose wife had no children, offered to take the girl home with him, together with part of the murderer's jewels. The sailor's wife was a good old soul and gave her a mother's love. "Poor dear, you will be our daughter!"

"You are such good people," said the girl. "I'm going to ask just one favour—let me always stay inside and be seen by no man."

"Don't worry, dear, nobody ever comes to our house."

The old man sold a few jewels and bought embroidery silk, so the girl spent her time embroidering. She made an exquisite tablecloth, working into it every colour and design under the sun, and the old woman took it to the nearby house of a king to sell.

"But who does this fine work?" asked the king.

"One of my daughters, Majesty," replied the old woman.

"Go on! That doesn't look like the work of a sailor's daughter," said the king, and bought the tablecloth.

The old woman used the money to buy more silk, and the girl embroidered a beautiful folding screen, which the old woman also took to the king.

"Is this really your daughter's work?" asked the king. He was still suspicious, and secretly followed her home.

Just as the old woman was closing the door, the king walked up and stuck his foot in it; the old woman let out a cry. Hearing the cry from her room, the girl thought the murderer had come after her and she fainted from fright. The old woman and the king came in and tried to revive her. She opened her eyes and, seeing that it was not the murderer, regained her senses.

"But what are you so afraid of?" asked the king, charmed with this girl.

"It's just my bad luck," she replied, and would say nothing more.

So the king started going to that house every day to keep the girl company and watch her embroider. He had fallen in love with her and finally asked for her hand in marriage. You can just imagine the old people's amazement. "Majesty, we are poor people," they began.

"No matter, I'm interested in the girl."

"I am willing," said the maiden, "but on one condition."

"What is that?"

"I refuse to see all men regardless of who they are, except you and my father." (She now called the old sailor her father.) "I will neither see them nor be seen by them."

The king consented to that. Jealous beyond measure, he was delighted she wanted to see no man but him.

Thus were they married in secret, so that no man would see her. The king's subjects were not at all happy over the matter, for when had a king ever married without showing the people his wife? The strangest of rumours began circulating. "He's married a monkey. He's married a hunchback. He's married a witch." Nor were the people the only ones to gossip; the highest dignitaries at the court also talked. So the king was forced to say to his wife, "You must appear in public for one hour and put an end to all those rumours."

The poor thing had no choice but obey. "Very well, tomorrow morning from eleven till noon I will appear on the terrace."

At eleven o'clock, the square was more packed than it had ever been. People had come from all over the country, even from the backwoods. The bride walked onto the terrace, and a murmur of admiration went up from the crowd. Never had they seen so beautiful a queen. She, however, scanned the crowd with uneasiness, and there in its midst stood a man cloaked in black. He brought his hand to his mouth and bit it in a threatening gesture, then held up his other arm, which ended in a stump. The queen sank to the ground in a swoon.

They carried her inside at once, and the old woman said over and over, "You would have to show her off! You would have to show her off against her will. Now just see what's happened!"

The queen was put to bed, and all the doctors were called in, but her illness baffled everyone. She insisted on remaining shut up and seeing no one, and she trembled all the time.

Meanwhile the king received a visit from a well-to-do foreign gentleman with a glib tongue and full of flattery. The king invited him to stay for dinner. The stranger, who was none other than the murderer, graciously accepted and ordered wine for everyone in the royal palace. Casks, barrels, and demijohns were brought in at once, but every drop of the wine had been drugged. That evening, guards, servants, ministers and everybody else drank their fill and, by night, they were dead drunk and snoring, the king loudest of all.

The murderer went through the palace making sure that on the stairs, in the corridors and all the rooms there was no one who wasn't flat on his back and sleeping. Then he tiptoed into the queen's room and found her hunched up in a corner of her bed and wide-eyed, almost as though she expected him.

"The hour has come for my revenge," hissed the murderer. "Get out of bed and fetch me a basin of water to wash the blood from my hands when I've cut your throat."

The queen ran out of the room to her husband. "Wake up! For heaven's sake, wake up!" But he slept on. Everybody in the whole palace slept, and there was no way in the world to wake them up. She got the basin of water and returned to her room.

"Bring me some soap, too," ordered the murderer as he sharpened his knife.

She went out, tried once more to rouse her husband, but to no avail. She then returned with the soap.

"And the towel?" asked the murderer.

She went out, got the pistol off of her sleeping husband, wrapped it in the towel and, making a motion to hand the towel to the murderer, fired a shot point-blank into his heart.

At that shot, the drunk people all woke up at the same time and, with the king in the lead, ran into her room. They found the murderer slain and the queen freed at last from her terror.

And another woman who saves herself! I wonder whether there once were many more tales like this, but as they were often collected by men, most of them were forgotten.

Powerful independent women are often assumed to be an invention of our modern times. But in the Middle Ages there was an astonishing number of female rulers, as men often managed to get themselves killed at quite an early age in wars and tournaments and it was quite common for their widows to inherit their power and position—a rule that a few centuries later would sound radical. Victorian ideas of what a woman should be were definitely less liberal than in those far older times. This tale from Florence may be proof of that. Of course, there is still the miser of a father, the power of the king and husband over our brave heroine's fate. Nevertheless the moral of the tale clearly is: women, don't trust your men to protect you. Take their pistols and do it yourself.

The Girl Who
Gave a Knight a
Kiss Out of
Necessity

Once there were some people who lived in a little house deep in the forest. They couldn't afford to keep a servant boy, but as luck would have it, they had a clever daughter who served as both girl and boy.

One time it happened that they had to take a sack of rye to be ground at the mill. They hoisted the bag onto the back of the horse, and the girl had to lead it there.

But when she'd gotten about halfway to the mill, the horse stumbled on a rock and the grain sack fell to the ground. She tried to hoist it back up on the horse, but it was too heavy and the horse wouldn't stand still.

While the girl stood there helplessly, a knight who was out hunting happened to pass by.

"Won't you please help me lift this sack up on the horse's back?" asked the girl when she saw the knight.

"Not unless you first give me a kiss," said the knight.

But the girl wouldn't do that; the sack could just lie there, she said to herself.

It was all the same to the knight, so he went on his way, and the girl was left standing there with her horse and sack.

But the knight liked her, for she was both beautiful and good, so he decided to test her again. He rode home, disguised himself in farmer's clothes, and at noontime came back to the girl in the forest.

"Good friend, won't you please help me put this sack of grain on the horse's back?" said the girl as soon as she saw the farmer.

"Not unless you first give me a kiss," said the farmer.

But the girl wouldn't do that; the sack would just have to lie there, she thought.

Well, that was all right with the farmer, and he went on his way. And the girl was left standing with her horse and her sack.

Now the knight thought even more highly of her, but he wanted to test her one more time. He went home, put on some old rags, smeared his face with soot, and slung a pack over his back so that he looked exactly like an old beggar. At sunset he came back to the girl in the forest.

"Dear old man, please help me put this sack back on the horse," said the girl when she saw the old beggar.

"Not unless you first give me a kiss," the old beggar said.

But the girl wouldn't do that. The sack could just lie there, she thought.

That was quite all right with the old beggar, and he started on his way.

The girl began to think that it would be pretty frightening to spend the whole night in the forest, so she made herself call him back and give him a kiss, no matter how much it embarrassed her.

In return, the old beggar helped her lift the sack onto the horse's back. Afterwards the girl went her way and the old man went his.

But the knight couldn't forget the lovely girl. He thought about her night and day, and it wasn't long before he appeared in the forest at the house of the old man and woman and asked for their daughter's hand. They were so surprised to receive such an honour that they neither dared nor wanted to object. And the girl, for her part, didn't mind marrying the rich and handsome knight. So they celebrated the wedding, and they ate so much that no one needed to be ashamed, and the girl moved in with the knight, and they lived so well that a king couldn't have lived any better.

Even so, the girl wasn't always happy. The knight spent too much time hunting, and he brought his hunting cronies home with him to the castle time and again. As you might guess, they led quite a life: beer and wine flowed from the barrels, and cups were passed around without stopping, and every one of them wanted to be wilder than his fellow.

As soon as the knight had enough to drink, he too became loud and talkative, and then he usually said:

"I know a girl who gave a knight a kiss out of necessity."

His drinking companions thought this very funny, and they laughed and leered and stared at the mistress for a long time, and the knight laughed and leered as well. The knight's words made her feel very sad.

One day the mistress's old godmother came to the castle enquiring about how her goddaughter was doing. Oh, well, everything was quite all right, said the mistress. But the old woman could see that everything was not as it should be, and she asked what the matter was. At first the mistress wouldn't say, but the old woman kept on asking until she told her.

"Maybe we can do something about that," she said, for she knew more than other people, she did.

A while afterwards the knight was out hunting. That day the forest seemed very strange, and the knight didn't recognize anything around him. Towards evening he wanted to ride home again, but he couldn't find his way. This was bad enough, of course, but even worse, he was getting very hungry; he hadn't eaten a crumb since morning. So he rode back and forth, back and forth, thinking that he'd find his way out, but it only grew wilder and darker around him. Finally, he spied a light and found his way to a little cottage. He got off the horse and went inside. There he saw an ugly old crone, who was setting a table with the most delicious-looking dishes.

"Splendid! Please allow me to buy a little food," the knight said very pleasantly.

"No," said the old crone, "I've no food for sale. But if you'll give me a kiss, you can have all you can eat."

"Ugh! Go to the Devil!" shouted the knight, and rushed out the door.

That was all right; the old crone didn't care one way or the other.

The knight jumped on his horse again. He'd rather forgo food for ever than kiss an ugly, toothless old crone. He rode and rode until the sweat poured off him and the horse, but he just couldn't get anywhere but to that poor little cottage. By now it was midnight and hunger was gnawing at his insides, so he tried the old crone again.

"You must let me buy a little food!" the knight pleaded.

"No," said the old crone, "I've no food for sale. But if you'll give me a kiss, you can eat as much as you want."

"Let the Devil kiss an old witch!" shouted the knight, and he rushed out the door again.

Very well—it didn't matter to the old crone.

The knight roamed about until far into the second day, and now and then the smell of the good food found its way to him. But he couldn't find his way out of the forest, and no matter what he did, he never got anywhere but to that horrible cottage. Finally, he had to take another turn with the old crone.

"Listen here, mother, you simply must let me buy a little food!" the knight demanded.

"No," said the old crone again, "I've no food for sale. But if you'll give me a kiss, you can have all you want."

"Like hell I will!" screamed the knight, and was about to rush out the door again.

Oh, but that was quite all right with the old crone.

Then the knight stopped and made himself calm down. Certainly, it was hard to imagine kissing such an ugly old lady, but he couldn't let himself starve to death either. Besides, no one but he ever needed to find out, for the old crone didn't know him, and he himself certainly wasn't going to speak about it. So he closed his eyes and gave her a kiss. Then she gave him food, as much as he wanted, and he made sure to take his full payment for that kiss. As soon as he got back into the forest, he had no trouble at all finding his way home.

Before long, his hunting companions came to visit the knight again, and wine and beer flowed as generously as before. Finally, the knight became so jolly that he started up with his old line: "I know a girl who gave a kiss to a knight out of necessity." He laughed, and his companions laughed too.

"And I know a knight who gave a kiss to an ugly, toothless old crone, just for some food," said the mistress.

Of course, it was her godmother who'd arranged the kiss, and she'd let the mistress know all about it.

Now there was even more laughing and shouting. But the knight only laughed and shouted a little, and thereafter no one ever spoke again of the girl who had to kiss a knight out of necessity.

Oh, I love this story. I discovered it only recently when I went through my fairy-tale books to find the right tales for this book. In far too many tales female characters are punished for their boldness and strength. Not here. Of course, Sweden as part of Scandinavia has a tradition of strong women—assuming it is true that the Vikings and most Germanic tribes had far less patriarchal ideas about their women. My childhood heroine Astrid Lindgren definitely added some unforgettable strong

girls to literature, Pippi Longstocking and Ronia the Robber's Daughter being the most famous ones.

But in this fairy tale there is not only the proud and strong-minded girl. Her godmother is clearly a white witch and the lesson she teaches the knight seems quite a modern one, which may mean that the tale is actually quite old. I once read a book about the lives of French noblewomen in the fourteenth century which taught me that their political power and freedom were often far beyond what women can claim today—a fact I already mentioned in my comment on The One-Handed Murderer.

Story Sources

The Boy Who Drew Cats
FROM JAPAN
Japanese Fairy Tales and Others retold by Lafcadio Hearn
(ISBN 9781602060715)
Pages 29–35

Kotura, Lord of the Winds
FROM SIBERIA
The Sun Maiden and the Crescent Moon—Siberian Folk Tales collected and translated by James Riordan
(ISBN 9780940793651)
Pages 59–67

Through the Water Curtain
FROM JAPAN
Japanese Tales translated by Royall Tyler (ISBN 9780375714511)
Pages 274–280

The Areca Tree
FROM VIETNAM
The Dragon Prince—Stories and Legends from Vietnam
by Thich Nhat Hanh (ISBN 9781888375749)
Pages 59–69

The Maid of the Copper Mountain
FROM RUSSIA
The Mistress of the Copper Mountain—Folk Tales from the Urals by Pavel Bazhov and retold by James Riordan (ISBN 9780584623918)
Pages 1–11

The Tale of the Firebird
FROM RUSSIA
The Tale of the Firebird retold and illustrated by Gennady Spirin and translated by Tatiana Popova (ISBN 9780399235849)

Bluebeard
FROM FRANCE
The Complete Fairy Tales by Charles Perrault, a new translation by Christopher Betts with illustrations by Gustave Doré (ISBN 9780199236831)
Pages 104–113

The Six Swans
FROM GERMANY
Brüder Grimm Kinder- und Hausmärchen, Ausgabe letzter Hand edited by Heinz Rölleke (ISBN 9783150531914)
Pages 251–256
Translated by Oliver Latsch

Golden Foot
FROM FRANCE
Französische Märchen—Volksmärchen des 19. und 20. Jahrhunderts edited by Ré Soupault (ISBN 9783828900431)
Pages 5–20
Translated by Oliver Latsch

The Story of One Who Set Out to Study Fear
FROM GERMANY
The Juniper Tree and Other Tales from Grimm, translated by Lore Segal and Randall Jarrell, and illustrated by Maurice Sendak (ISBN 9780374339715)
Pages 23–41

The Frog Princess
FROM UKRAINE
The Magic Egg and Other Tales from Ukraine retold by Barbara J. Suwyn, edited and introduced by Natalie O. Kononenko (ISBN 9781563084256)
Pages 122–131

The One-Handed Murderer
FROM ITALY
Italian Folktales selected and retold by Italo Calvino
(ISBN 9780156454896)
Pages 328–332

The Girl Who Gave a Knight a Kiss Out of Necessity
FROM SWEDEN
Swedish Folktales and Legends edited by Lone Thygesen
Blecher and George Blecher (ISBN 9780679758419)
Pages 257–260

CORNELIA FUNKE is one of the bestselling children's writers in the world. Her books have sold tens of millions of copies, and they include the *Inkheart* trilogy, *Dragon Rider*, *The Thief Lord* and the *Reckless* series, which is published by Pushkin Press. Cornelia has long been inspired by fairy tales from around the world.

Cornelia Funke Titles
Published by Pushkin Press

THE RECKLESS SERIES:

THE GLASS OF LEAD AND GOLD

PUSHKIN CHILDREN'S BOOKS

We created Pushkin Children's Books to share tales from different languages and cultures with younger readers, and to open the door to the wide, colourful worlds these stories offer.

From picture books and adventure stories to fairy tales and classics, and from fifty-year-old bestsellers to current huge successes abroad, the books on the Pushkin Children's list reflect the very best stories from around the world, for our most discerning readers of all: children.

THE BEGINNING WOODS
MALCOLM MCNEILL

'I loved every word and was envious of quite a few... A modern classic. Rich, funny and terrifying'
Eoin Colfer

THE RED ABBEY CHRONICLES
MARIA TURTSCHANINOFF

1 · *Maresi*
2 · *Naondel*

'Embued with myth, wonder, and told with a dazzling, compelling ferocity'
Kiran Millwood Hargrave, author of *The Girl of Ink and Stars*

THE LETTER FOR THE KING
TONKE DRAGT

'*The Letter for the King* will get pulses racing... Pushkin Press deserves every praise for publishing this beautifully translated, well-presented and captivating book'
The Times

THE SECRETS OF THE WILD WOOD
TONKE DRAGT

'Offers intrigue, action and escapism'
Sunday Times

THE SONG OF SEVEN
TONKE DRAGT

'A cracking adventure... so nail-biting you'll need to wear protective gloves'
The Times

THE MURDERER'S APE
JAKOB WEGELIUS

'A thrilling adventure. Prepare to meet the remarkable Sally Jones; you won't soon forget her'
Publishers Weekly

THE PARENT TRAP · THE FLYING CLASSROOM · DOT AND ANTON

ERICH KÄSTNER

Illustrated by Walter Trier

'The bold line drawings by Walter Trier are the work of genius... As for the stories, if you're a fan of *Emil and the Detectives*, then you'll find these just as spirited'

Spectator

FROM THE MIXED-UP FILES OF MRS. BASIL E. FRANKWEILER

E. L. KONIGSBURG

'Delightful... I love this book... a beautifully written adventure, with endearing characters and full of dry wit, imagination and inspirational confidence'

Daily Mail

THE RECKLESS SERIES

CORNELIA FUNKE

1 · *The Petrified Flesh*
2 · *Living Shadows*
3 · *The Golden Yarn*

'A wonderful storyteller'

Sunday Times

THE WILDWITCH SERIES

LENE KAABERBØL

1 · *Wildfire*
2 · *Oblivion*
3 · *Life Stealer*
4 · *Bloodling*

'Classic fantasy adventure... Young readers will be delighted to hear that there are more adventures to come for Clara'

Lovereading

MEET AT THE ARK AT EIGHT!

ULRICH HUB

Illustrated by Jörg Mühle

'Of all the books about a penguin in a suitcase pretending to be God asking for a cheesecake, this one is absolutely, definitely my favourite'

Independent

THE SNOW QUEEN

HANS CHRISTIAN ANDERSEN

Illustrated by Lucie Arnoux

'A lovely edition [of a] timeless story'

The Lady

THE WILD SWANS

HANS CHRISTIAN ANDERSEN

'A fresh new translation of these two classic fairy tales recreates the lyrical beauty and pathos of the Danish genius' evergreen stories'

The Bay

THE CAT WHO CAME IN OFF THE ROOF

ANNIE M.G. SCHMIDT

'Guaranteed to make anyone 7-plus to 107 who likes to curl up with a book and a cat purr with pleasure'

The Times

LAFCADIO: THE LION WHO SHOT BACK

SHEL SILVERSTEIN

'A story which is really funny, yet also teaches us a great deal about what we want, what we think we want and what we are no longer certain about once we have it'

Irish Times

THE SECRET OF THE BLUE GLASS

TOMIKO INUI

'I love this book... How important it is, in these times, that our children read the stories from other peoples, other cultures, other times'

Michael Morpurgo, *Guardian*

THE STORY OF THE BLUE PLANET

ANDRI SNÆR MAGNASON

Illustrated by Áslaug Jónsdóttir

'A Seussian mix of wonder, wit and gravitas'

The New York Times